John Williams

Poems by the Late John Williams

John Williams

Poems by the Late John Williams

ISBN/EAN: 9783337401504

Printed in Europe, USA, Canada, Australia, Japan

Cover: Foto ©Andreas Hilbeck / pixelio.de

More available books at **www.hansebooks.com**

POEMS,

BY THE LATE

JOHN WILLIAMS.

EDITED BY HIS SON,

THOMAS WILLIAMS.

LONDON:

H. SOTHERAN & CO., 10, LITTLE TOWER STREET, E.C.

1873.

CONTENTS.

—

MEMOIR OF JOHN WILLIAMS.

BY THE EDITOR.

——:o:——

My father, the author of the poems comprised in this volume, was the son of James and Margaret Williams; and was born at Lecha, in the parish of St. Just-in-Penwith, Cornwall, in the year 1808. His youth was, however, principally passed at Tregaseal, to which neighbouring village his parents removed while he was yet a child. Being one of numerous brothers and sisters, and his father, although a most respectable man,—who was once offered, but declined, a mine "captaincy," or supervisorship,—being poor, the education which he received in boyhood was, necessarily, of a very limited character; and was chiefly imparted to him by the parish clerk, Mr. Thomas Tregear. At an early age he left school, and forthwith obtained employment at one of the mines, which, in some way or other, engage the services of so large a proportion of the population of Cornwall.

An assistant at the same mine, was a lad, of about his own age, named John Thomas, between whom and himself there soon sprang up an intimacy, that ultimately ripened into an ardent friendship, which lasted

throughout the remainder of their joint lives. "It was
here,"—writes the survivor of the youths, in a letter
which I have lately received from him,—"that the starting
point in our lives, religious and mental, originated.
Thus: one Monday afternoon, we were alone in the mine.
Our conversation was, at first, such as might be expected
from two boys,—our age was about fourteen years.—Soon,
however, a feeling of seriousness took possession of our
minds; and it resulted in our, there and then, on our
knees, unseen by mortal eye, vowing to consecrate our
lives to God, and His Church. That vow, by the grace of
God, was never violated."

Forthwith, the lads renounced the society of such of their
companions as were evil-disposed, and on the following
Sunday entered into Christian fellowship. They now,
also, commenced together a course of reading and study.
But I cannot do better than continue Mr. Thomas' own
narrative of this part of my father's life. "At that
time," says he, "about the year 1822, books were scarce,
and very dear. Our parents had large families to provide
for, and but little money to spare for books. Our
difficulties were many and formidable. Through a religious
agency, we obtained, once a month, a couple of juvenile
magazines from London; I don't remember that we had
any other periodicals at that time. There was a society
connected with the chapel, consisting of a small number
of members, who paid twopence or threepence a month

for the loan of a book.   Of this, also, we availed ourselves ; and from these two limited sources it was that your father drew almost the only aid he obtained in the pursuit of knowledge, "under difficulties," indeed. Very many of the books thus procured, we literally devoured : —I have a list of them by me to the present time.— Your father committed to memory nearly the whole of Thomson's "Seasons," Burns' Poems, and Scott's Poems. He could recite all of "The Lady of the Lake."   Boswell's Life of Johnson, too. in four volumes, he had at heart ; could repeat any anecdote, or incident, in the work. Foster's "Essays," the "Rambler," Chalmers' "Astronomy," and "Religion," "Locke's Essay on the Understanding," Dr. Watts' "Logic," and "Improvement of the Mind." &c., &c., he devoured, I may say. Poetry was his delight. He committed thousands upon thousands of lines to memory.   In fact, literary work engaged his mind at all times, as far as the duties of religion, and daily employment gave him opportunity. I ought to add, that no consideration, personal pleasure, or literary studies, ever interfered with, or unduly absorbed, religious duties. His mental characteristic was metaphysical.

"Perhaps, you would like to have a few ideas in connection with his youthful habits, and efforts to emerge from the obscurity of his position. He was indebted. more than to anything else, for his advancement, to the following:—I told you that, as soon as we decided upon a

religious life, we abandoned all boyish trifling, and set
about self-improvement. Very soon after entering into
Church fellowship, we were employed in various offices in
connection therewith. Every evening we could meet, we
did so, and, after fulfilling our regular duties at meetings,
&c., we took rambles into solitary localities, away from
observation as much as possible. During these lonely
walks, which sometimes extended to midnight, we exer-
cised ourselves in questions of science, history, theology,
&c., having only one end in view,—self-improvement.
These nightly discussions provided thought for the
intervening time between the next meeting ; which
thought, we, as often as possible, committed to writing,
exchanging papers at our next interview. My conviction
is, that my friend, as well as myself, were indebted for
the future advantages we obtained, socially and inter-
lectually, to these meetings.

" Our native village was "remote and unfriendly " to
minds like ours. Thus : we had no bookseller nearer than
Penzance, seven miles distant ; and many a time did we
walk thither for the purpose of getting a book, or of
hearing a lecture on phiiosophy, &c., and walk home
again at night, sometimes at midnight."

The evening rambles "into solitary localities" to which
Mr. Thomas has alluded, are referred to in the first poem
in this volume ; as, also, in the verses " To a friend,"
which are addressed to himself.

Mr. Thomas adds, that both my father and he were accustomed, at the earliest period of their acquaintance, " to engage in reciprocal efforts at versification, in an unpretending manner" at their social interviews.

In further reference to the extraordinarily studious habits of the author, the following incident is related by his surviving sisters. One afternoon, my father left the mine rather earlier than usual. He had not reached his parents' house, however, by the accustomed bed-time ; and the family retired to rest without him. In the night, his mother dreamt that she saw some one being borne from the mine in an apparently lifeless state ; and she started up, affrighted, and enquired if " John" had come home. Being answered in the negative, a fear seized her, and presently communicated itself to all the members of the household, that some dreadful accident had befallen him. Whereupon, his brother dressed himself, and went out in search of my father, whom he eventually discovered at the house of his inseparable student-friend, at close study ; and, although it was then three o'clock in the morning, the young men were indifferent alike to fatigue, hunger, and the advancing dawn, in their ardent pursuit after knowledge.

At this date, there resided in St. Just two remarkable men, viz.; Messrs. John Davy and Richard Oats. The former was parish schoolmaster, the latter tin-dresser ; and both, though self-taught, were possessed of excellent

mental attainments, particularly excelling in mathematical
knowledge, in which science, Mr. Davy, indeed, was a
distinguished proficient. As soon as Messrs. Davy and
Oats got to hear of the two young men's thirst for learning, they assisted them with their aid,—directing their
studies, and lending them books, with much advantage
to the students. Towards these early benefactors, my father
always retained a feeling of deep indebtedness ; and,
throughout the remainder of his life, invariably spoke of
them with the utmost esteem and affection. They both
died many years before him, and my father commemo-
rated the decease of Mr. Davy in a poem, which is
printed in this volume. He also wrote, not long before
his own final illness, a prose article, entitled, "The Old
School Room," in which Mr. Davy figures as the hero.
That article is reproduced at the end of this memoir.
While, of Mr. Oats my father said, in a letter referring
to that gentleman's death, in 1842. " Have not the ranks
of literature, and the lovers of learning, lost in him an
advocate for the truth, one in whom there was blended,
with rare abilities, great discrimination ; who was not to
be imposed upon by mere specious reasoning, or the tinsel
and show of superficial acquirement ? He thought for
himself, he examined for himself; and withstood, with
becoming tenacity, every departure from the boundary of
real evidence, and every innovation on the laws of argu-
ment, and sound philosophy. Yet, but few men enjoyed

a greater luxury in the realization of truth, or gave themselves up with greater willingness to acknowledge, to receive, and to applaud it."

It was but natural that two young men of the habits of Mr. Thomas and my father, should soon find a sphere more suited to their talents than that in which they were originally placed. The former early attained, and still occupies, an honourable and dignified position at Manchester ; and my father, having first, for a year or two, acted as village schoolmaster, procured a junior clerkship in the service of Mr. John Batten, Penzance, one of the most respected of merchants and of residents in Cornwall; and in that gentleman's employ he remained until the date of his death,—a period of over thirty years ; —having, for a considerable while prior to his decease, to a great extent managed Mr. Batten's business. My father died in 1866, of congestion of the lungs, after a long and prostrating illness, endured with much Christian fortitude. My mother, whom he married soon after his removal to Penzance, and who proved one of the most affectionate and conscientious of wives, as she was one of the most affectionate and conscientious of parents, had died five years before.

He lies buried in the Penzance Cemetery ; having been laid, at his expressed desire, in the Church of England portion of that enclosure. Mr. Prebendary Hedgeland, Incumbent of St. Mary's, Penzance, with whom my father,

during his final illness, enjoyed several religious conversa-
tions, conducted his funeral service.

Although the author held, as will be seen, a position of
trust·and respectability, and was much esteemed by those
who knew him, he was not, on the whole, so successful
in life as his talents warranted.   He was too modest and
retiring a man to impress with his capabilities any
persons but those who were his intimate friends.   "I
verily believe," he wrote, at the age of forty, "more than
half the world is ahead of me!" This conviction does not
seem, however, to have distressed him much ; for he soon
afterwards adds (but) "if one is not the headmost, there
is, certainly, a flattering unction in the thought that one
is not at the tail end of the host."   Probably, too, he
was sustained by the reflection that the noblest prizes,
even of this life, are not of a visible and material kind;
nay, more,—that, as a rule, people cannot win both re-
wards, inward peace, and outward prosperity ; which, as
F. W. Robertson expresses it, would be to "come back,
like Joseph's brethren from the land of plenty, with the
corn in their sacks, and the money returned, too, in
their sacks' mouths."

Beyond filling some Church offices ; delivering a few
lectures before the Literary Institutes of Penzance and
St. Just ; and occasionally taking part in the discussions
of the former society, my father scrupulously shunned
publicity of any sort.   He was, however, a fair speaker,

although that same diffidence to which I have referred prevented his manner from doing justice to his matter, either as a lecturer, or a debater. His matter, indeed, was generally good, whether he appeared in the capacities just mentioned ; as a conversationist, or a writer. For he possessed an original and reflective mind ; was always a great reader, and retained most that he read. He had a mellow voice, and was a capital reciter of poetry, particularly plaintive poetry, which he repeated with most touching pathos. He was intensely fond of music, especially vocal music ; and, himself, sang tenor well.

He was much given to country walks ; was an admirer of trees, and flowers, and simple peasant-life. He was also a lover of children ; and frequently engaged in conversation, nor seldom in play, with small boys and girls whom he had happened to meet in his rambles. Indeed, not one of his poems recalls his form so vividly to my recollection as that entitled " Little Children."

Mr. Thomas has described that my father, even in his boyhood, attempted poetical composition. The earliest printed poem of his with which I am acquainted, is one entitled " A Sunday School Scholar's Address to a Congregation," which is an appeal on behalf of that institution, written for, and spoken by, one of the children at the Sunday school with which the author was connected in his youth.

I quote a few lines of the poem; with its very practical termination.

> " Shall we in vain implore your bounteous aid, —
> On whom our claims for guardianship are laid ?
> We urge our plea: by nature's stubborn ties
> We are your offspring, then regard our cries.
> Behold these youths, that fain your aid would prove ;
> And let for us compassion's bowels move.
> Cast on your mercy, can ye slight our claim ?
> Or act unworthy of the Christian name ?
> Can England's philanthropic current cease
> For native youths ?   For us can it decrease,
> While from our shores its endless blessings roll,
> From East to West, from North to Southern pole ?
> Can ye,—the people of a Christian land,—
> Can Christians' ears, and hearts, our plea withstand ?
> No !   While these institutions grace our isle,
> You'll give your efforts,—heaven on them will smile.
> Then let the spells of charity entwine,
> And touch your hearts, as with a power divine.
>
> Now, let your hearts, hands, pockets, all unite ;
> And in the treasury cast ye, all, your mite."

The author was, probably, about nineteen, or twenty years of age when these lines were written. At this time, and for many years afterwards, he seems to have given much of his attention to poetical composition. Indeed the greater portion of the poems contained in this volume, as well as a large number of pieces that are not included in the present collection, were written while the author was a young man.   I am not aware that any of the verses so composed were ever contributed to a publication.   Several of the poems were, however, printed, and privately circulated in the form of a pamphlet, by the author, in the year 1858. Most of the remainder of the verses contained in this volume were written in the latter part of the year 1860, and the beginning of the year 1861, after my father had for many years forsaken the muse.   They were composed with,—for the author, who usually elaborated very much,—remarkable rapidity ; and were contributed anonymously,—I have said that my father always shunned publicity,—to the columns of the "Cornish Telegraph," one of the oldest journals in the West of England, and one which has numbered on its staff of occasional writers not a few Cornishmen of distinction, among whom, —to quote only two recent instances,—are Mr. J. T. Blight, F.S.A. the well known Artist-antiquary, and my friend Mr. W. Bottrell, whose first series of "Traditions and Hearthside Stories of West Cornwall" met with so cordial a reception a few years ago ; and who has just issued the second series of those interesting and valuable contributions to legendary lore.

The poems which the author composed in 1860-1,

certainly include many of his best, comprising, as they do,
" Little Children," " The Old Soldier," " To the Daisy,"
" To the Primrose," " Departed Hours," " 'Tis Summer
Time," and " To a Thrush." The old poetic spirit was now
strong on my father ; and he might, doubtless, at this
time, have written pieces of greater merit than even the
beautiful productions which I have named : but the
illness, and decease, of my mother, which latter event
occurred in November, 1861, so shocked his sensitive
frame, that, although he survived his sad loss five years,
he never afterwards composed a single line of poetry. To
the last he felt keenly my mother's death. Thus : writing
to me in 1865, four years after its occurrence, he says
with obvious reference thereto, " we shall be glad to
welcome you home. The word brings tears to my eyes !
It is not home as it once was."

Although my father joined himself, in early life, to one
of the most exclusive of religious fraternities, and, despite
a strong attachment to the Church of England, continued
in the community of the former body to the date of his
death, he was not in the least degree tainted by, but, on the
contrary, was a constant critic of, the "clannishness" which,
he considered, was one of the worst features of his denomi-
nation. He was also a warm opponent of the sanctimo-
nious school of theology. Thus : writing to me in 1865,
respecting a certain minister, then located at Penzance,
he says : "W— improves, and, with me, and many like me,

is rather a favourite. He is a liberal, unsectarian,
common-sense man, and an interesting preacher: but is not
quite "straight" enough for the Puritan class. He quotes
in his sermons, and, often, happily enough, from Shakespeare,
Byron, Shelley, Moore, Burns, or any body else." I am
not prepared to say that my father belonged, by sympathy,
to the Broad Church. He had, however, a strong
antipathy to the Narrow Church, which, as Dr. Wendell
Holmes so forcibly describes it, " may be seen in the ship's
boats of humanity ; in the long boat, in the jolly boat, in
the captain's gig, lying off the poor old vessel, thanking
God that *they* are safe, and reckoning how soon the hulk
containing the mass of their fellow creatures will go down:"
and he was, certainly, " very slow to believe that the ship
will be swallowed up, with so many poor people in it,
fastened down under the hatches ever since it floated."
But, in my father's case, any unwillingness to subscribe
to all the doctrines of, what is called, orthodoxy, did not
proceed from either of those two common causes of ultra
Broad Churchism in the present day; viz. in the first
place, the disagreement of the practise with certain pure
precepts which are then discarded, as being a constant pro-
test against the life lived,—the creed being thus conformed to
the conduct, instead of the conduct to the creed:—and, in
the second place, that pride of intellect, usually a very
shallow intellect, which, because one's religion is, to a
great extent, a thing of tradition, on that very account

rejects its tenets as "grandmother's tales;" as though, admitting that the doctrines handed down to us by our ancestors are not, therefore, necessarily true, it followed that they were, therefore, necessarily false. The life which my father lived, and the death which he died, both attest that none of his views had any such origin; which will easily be credited by the reader of the following poems, so full of the warmest religious feeling:—poems, be it observed, that were written so little for the public eye that most of those persons who were acquainted with the author in his life time were unaware that he ever composed a single line of poetry.

My father was a good writer of prose, as well as of verse; and was an excellent epistolary correspondent. He wrote long letters, full of news, and most of them embodying some original reflections, bearing on religion, on philosophy, and on the practical duties of life. Indeed, from his articles, his lectures, and his letters, it would not be difficult for an intrinsically interesting volume to be compiled. In the present instance. I content myself, however, with reproducing simply two articles in illustration of my father's literary style. The last of these, to which I have already referred, possesses an independent value, as being a prose supplement to the author's poetical tribute to the worth of his revered friend, Mr. Davy.

Writing to Mr. Thomas, in 1848, my father,—after

expressing it as his opinion that, in life, "the world will do justice to us;" that "if we are pleased, and are pleasing to others, we shall, certainly, make a soft place for ourselves, and, bad as the world is, when we fall, the crowd will not trample upon us,"—says, "Nor am I sure it is * * wrong in us to hope for the world's benediction, even at the winding-up of the drama: for it seems to be desirable, as the last rites are being performed for us, and we are about to be huddled out of sight, to have one's name coupled with a blessing, and one's memory embalmed in the affections of the living. And, in this respect also, I verily believe the world will not deal with us unjustly, but will be as faithful in death as in life * * * Depend upon it, we shall suffer no wrong."

The world, as represented by that small portion of it which knew my father in his life-time, proved itself, in his case, thus just, as he had anticipated. He died amid general respect for his moral excellencies; of which, if I ever had the slightest doubt on the point, the letters that have been addressed to me during the passage through the press of the present work would have fully assured me. And I am in hope that even his intellectual qualities, which the world is not to be censured for not discovering while he lived, seeing that he carefully concealed them from the popular gaze, will, through the publication of this little volume, now, also meet with their due meed of recognition.

BOYHOOD.

[By Pater Familias.]

CHRISTMAS is that season of the year in which the family-circle, still of blessed memory, usually receives a very agreeable accession to its members. Then it is that we greet once more the faces of old and valued friends; and children from school, or from the different spheres in which they are placed, are again here, with cheerful countenances, tinged, we hope, with rosy health; and, we may safely say, with hearts brim-full of joy,—a joy which none but those we are speaking of can feel. We can only remember it. Describe it we may; or, at least, attempt it: feel it we cannot, in all its freshness, as once we did. The stern realities of later life, and a few steps in advance of you, O juveniles! on the way, have now seared the warm and plastic texture of our school-boy heart and nature, and rendered them impervious, in some degree, to the bliss which is peculiarly your own. Nor has *Tom Brown's School days*, with its inimitable and graphic humour, manliness, and honesty, been yet able to restore the old feeling, and again kindle the original flame. Had it been in the power of any mere book to accomplish this, Tom, certainly, would have achieved the task.

The nearest approach to such feelings as we are now

speaking of has, we think, been effected on revisiting the old, and ever-to-be-remembered *School-room* of our boyhood,—a place sanctified by time, and a thousand cherished remembrances. It stands within the area of the churchyard-wall of our native place ; and may, therefore, be described as a part and parcel of the venerable edifice. In reality, it is only separated from it by a thin partition. It is, therefore, needless to say that hard-by, and around it, repose the dust of ages, the remains of many of our school-fellows, and the bones of our forefathers. And, ashamed should we be of ourselves, were not that alone sufficient to give it a tenfold interest. Of this, however, we thought little, as, with boyish hilarity, we bounded through its low-arched door-way, at the Christmas vacation, —unharnessed, for a while, from school restraint,—and took our leave of the revered preceptor, a man, indeed, of cheerful and agreeable demeanour, beloved by all, and of very considerable attainments. Had we to follow in the wake of Tom Brown, we should select him for our hero.

Rugby itself, with all its paraphernalia, so graphically sketched, never came with more of the omnipotence of an irresistible enchantment upon Tom Brown's heart than the associations which this old *School-room* has awakened in our own. Visiting it, in recent years, with a foot, or more, added to the perpendicular dimension of the system, we

have had to enter the low Gothic doorway with the body
brought to a considerable curve, at least to an angle of
a few degrees. In our boyhood, we thought this entrance
as high as needs be. And the old tower,—grey with age,
—looks now really nothing in height compared with the
view which our youthful imagination presented.

Without digressing farther from what, at first, we in-
tended to say, you, who are now, for awhile, freed from
school restraint, and are again safely housed beneath the
paternal roof, may well look cheerful and happy ; and
though, as we before said, we cannot participate with you
in all that you feel, yet we would augment your felicity
by every means in our power. At least, we greet you with
the compliments of the season, and do indeed wish you, and
yours, happiness and prosperity in this life, and, beyond,
the felicity of a better. It should be to you a source of
no little enjoyment that, while many a poor youth is
houseless and homeless, and their hearts withering with
vice and anguish, you have the shelter of a home, and the
paternal welcome awaiting you ; that you can again
nestle down in the sunshine of that maternal heart whose
sympathies for you we cannot describe. Nor is it always
to be placed to the account of youth, if it is not so.
Parents who are constantly churlish and ill-tempered, forget
how often they exclude the sunlight from the domestic

atmosphere. In their presence there is perpetual shade. Far be it from us to be dictatory. We would rather admonish ; and we say, with deference to the judgment of others, better relax in the rugged and sterner virtues, and let the heart thaw into real, warm, benevolent feeling, good humour, and cheerfulness,—a demeanour dictated alike by self-interest and the relations of life in which we are placed.

We think it a capital trait, and indicative of nobleness of heart, and the possession of true good-humour, when a father is seen among the juveniles "leaping the long mare," or "hunting the slipper." Or, if you prefer it, by all means get down on all fours, with your Johnny or your Jimmy mounted aloft, or both at the same time, if you can get fairly round the room before you give in. And if you do fall, with the urchins rolling you, half stifled, on the floor, get up, laugh it right out, and try again. We quite agree with the writer on muscular Christianity. And it may be questioned whether the world is much the better for the development of the demurer graces. For cheerfulness and good humour ever stand associated with the noblest qualities of human character. And religion and virtue themselves are seldom attractive where these are not seen.

THE OLD SCHOOL-ROOM.

[*By Pater Familias.*]

We did not tell you,— juvenile readers, or any other readers,—in our last week's remarks on Boyhood, that there was anything more on Boyhood in the back ground to invite attention respecting the OLD SCHOOL-ROOM, to which we then merely alluded. Nor are we quite convinced, even in our own mind, that, in this said background, there will be found sufficient material to analyze, and work-up into anything like readable matter. For we cannot expect the juvenile portion of the community, who are passing through the educational process, to be much interested in anything that may be addressed to them on such a subject, especially at this season of the year, when the name of *School-room* may very likely be to them the most insipid and objectionable of all imaginable words. And yet, after all,—speaking from experience,—we think there must ever be a great deal connected with an old *School-room* calculated to interest most individuals, and to awaken lively recollections of the past,—the never-to-be-forgotten old spot, where the first sight of a numeration table met our youthful eyes, and looked so much like a simple musical instrument with which we had been familiar, namely, a triangle, that it inspired pleasing recollections, and suggested the idea of easy conquest. We liked its appearance because, begining within a small space at the top, we at once saw that we were to descend, by very gentle steps, to a much wider base ; a process much easier, certainly, than going upward. From this commencement, to the winding up of the whole course, what a field opens up in retrospect! We soon found it was not a downward process upon which we had entered. For, the oblique, ladder-shaped appearance of the sums in long division, and the difficulty we found in working them correctly, caused us many a sigh and severe mental struggle ; and early engendered in our youthful minds a deeply rooted hatred of that rule. But, nothwithstanding all this, the old *School-room* brings with it a thousand cherished remembrances.

Who, as he grasps the hand of an old school-fellow, after years and years have rolled by, does not feel a thrill of emotion, and his heart beat quicker? What a broad space in our brief history is, in a moment, laid open ! And, ere the hand relaxes its warm grasp, and the eye is turned from the countenance that meets our own, the mind sweeps backward over the past,—over many years of toil and travel,—and, in spite of anything we can oppose to it, every nook and corner of the old *School-room*,—bench, and desk, and forms, and the faces, too, that once were there, —are again distinctly visible in our imagination.

But there is one figure in that group more commanding, more interesting, than all beside. It stands out in bold relief ; and with it are blended many recollections. The head, gently bent, as if in thoughtful mood, is blanched with the flight of years. The countenance, naturally bland, open, and pleasing, is alternately lighted with a smile as some happy idea, or clue to the solution of the all-absorbing question, is suggested to the mind. And the deep lines of thought in the ample forehead are distinctly visible. The twilight of a November's evening is stealing through the old mullioned windows, coeval, we believe, with the grey old tower, hard by, that has stood unmoved amid the storms of ages, a memento of past generations.

The impatient fellows within, awaiting their dismissal at half-past four o'clock, are eying stealthily the venerated preceptor, hoping he will soon wake-up to the consciousness of the outer world of sport, and the approach of the hour of separation for the day. At length, all is bustle and momentary confusion, as each one is anxious to escape, and the old *School-room*,—cleared of its occupants save one,—is joyfully left behind. "Save one," did we say? Yes! and he is to spend many hours there ere he, too, will quit it. In the field of mathematical science he is no mere stripling; no showy pretender. He is, truly, a mathematician of the first water; and, in general attainment, though self-taught, will rank above most men even of liberal education. There are before him, even yet, full six hours of mental toil in his favourite pursuit. Outside. are seen the pupils in active amusement, straining muscle and limb; or scattered in groups over the sacred enclosure, for the church-yard was oft the play ground. And some grave-stone that has, or has not, yet been surmounted, as the case may be, is the object of general attention; to pass clear over which is the universal ambition. Or, more important still was the experiment of placing the left foot against the base of the old tower, and flinging a stone right up, in a straight direction, to the top, sheer over turret and pinnacle. And, among that group, there were stout fellows, strong in muscle and limb : for we must tell you that, in those days, and in that rural district, boys really had muscles and limbs.

But there is another part of the picture yet to be looked at. The shades of night have wrapped in oblivion all surrounding objects. The hour of midnight is fast

approaching, and silence is reigning undisturbed, in awful
and impressive grandeur. We take our stand on the public
thoroughfare, at a little distance from the old *School-
room*, and opposite to it. A faint light is gleaming
through the small panes of the old Gothic windows, and
shedding a feeble ray on the grave-stones around, standing
erect, like so many sentinels keeping watch over the
slumberers beneath. Yes! the light is there. In that
old *School-room*, it has shone forth for five hours, at least ;
and the indefatigable man is plodding his way through
the mazes of abstruse science, mindless of the outer world,
and earning for himself an honourable reputation.

How strong in the human breast is the desire for knowledge, and how deeply seated it is in the heart of him who
is truly initiated in the ways of science ! The clock has
struck the 'midnight hour, and still the light is gleaming
forth,—pale, feeble and sickly. Outside, are the living
and the dead, locked in slumber. Not so the watcher
within. His eye brightens with inward delight as he ex-
plores, and demonstrates to a certainty, the great truths
of science ; to him, clear as the noon-day beam. His con-
clusions are no baseless suppositions, hastily arrived at,
doubtful, and uncertain ; but sure and evident. He feels he
is standing on solid ground, firm as the pillars of the earth.
But, you will ask, wherefore is the labour undertaken ?

And why is it that a man thus toils in the thorny paths of science ? The answer is at hand. It brings its own reward. The rational delight which a man feels in demonstrating great truths is known only to himself. Permit us also to remind you that the first of May is approaching,—the latest period allowed by the Editor of the *Lady's Diary*, a work of a gone-by period, for receiving the contributions of correspondents. And the name of him of whom we are now speaking stands connected with its pages, as the author and solver of some of the most beautiful and masterly questions inserted in the mathematical department of that annual repository. This work is now published under the title of *The Lady's and Gentleman's Diary.*

Time, on its ever-moving pinions, has borne us onward, amid the jostlings of life's journey, through many years of change. We come unexpectedly, yet agreeably, in contact with one who is our fellow traveller. Many vicissitudes have occurred in our respective histories since we last sat side by side, in our teens, in that *old School-room*, no matter where. Half doubtingly, we ask ourselves are we the same ? Let us scan each other's features. Can we trace any resemblance to former identity ? We can. But time, with all the incidents in its train, has done its work. He is much altered in appearance. The ardour and vivacity of boyhood are exchanged for the soberness and gravity of more than middle life. But, a few words only are spoken before we mark the same shrewd, discriminating look. It is there as it ever was. Yes, the same firm grey eye is yet there, though now a little shrunk, and widening the contrast between itself and that bold, projecting forehead, width and fulness of temple, which phrenologists would label with the word "number." Yes, he was the pale-complexioned little fellow, far from tall for his age, but strongly-shaped, diligent, open, good tempered; our main stay in difficulties, our secret, but not the less our generous, friend; a little in advance of us in age, and much our superior in all things except marbles. If there was a warm and unbroken friendship cemented, is that to be wondered at? When was it in your school-boy history that you had not a friend; a sort of guide, companion, and daily arbitrator, to whom all differences were submitted; one well acquainted with your signal of distress, whether it was a soft whisper, or a fixed and imploring look; and one who never failed to render assistance when you had lost your reckoning, and were drifting in a wrong direction? Had you never such a friend? We anticipate the answer. And have you, or have you not, forgotten that stout-limbed, square-built, big-shouldered, fair-complexioned boy that sat opposite you at the same desk?

We remember such, and also that we had the honour of being pitted against him in the process of oblique lines and pot-hooks ; and remember, too, the hope we entertained of soon outstripping him, after observing that the poor fellow had actually lost two of the fingers of his right hand. But, do we remember how often in our life time we have found that, by what Sir Walter Scott has called

'The will to do, the soul to dare'

difficulties are overcome, and natural defects are more than counter-balanced, by acquired habits ! He was really a diligent, determined, high-mettled fellow, with whom to stand even a comparison at the next Christmas vacation was a task we were not at all anxious for.

How many histories and incidents are there, in connection with the *old School-room*, that stand out in the long distance of the past as mementoes to remind us of the abbreviated space that lies beyond ! How often will they rise up in retrospect, round which the memory yet lingers, we hope with some degree of satisfaction ! It is by no means a desirable condition when we cannot dwell on our school-boy history without much self-reproach. Nor do we envy the self-accusing reflections of that ever-detested, big, bronze-faced fellow, who was always wanting to mix, and chafe, and cheat, and bully, among his

juniors, had never the courage to face his equal ; and
was sure to make off when he was a winner in the game.
and when the odds were against him in a quarrel.   You
may be sure that school-boys had their quarrels in those
days, as well as in the present ; and, as a matter of
course, you will say the weaker had to suffer.   Nay, it
was not always so.   Frequently, there were some noble
fellows, honest enough, manly enough, and able enough
to defend the right, and who, when present, never failed
to do so.   Don't we all remember such worthies ? We do :
and, although we cannot now stand face to face with
many of them, yet we greet the remembrance of their names.
And, if there are sympathies existing between the spiritual
natures of the visible and invisible world,—a doctrine by
no means to be discarded,—then, perhaps, we are not to
ascribe entirely to natural causes that inward sighing,
deep emotion, and fulness of the heart we sometimes
experience when the memory of a departed friend is again
revived, and the solemn scene of removal is again re-pass-
ing before us.   It was painful to see poor Harry's seat in
the *old School-room* vacant, ever honest and noble-hearted
as he was. And a saddening interview was that to undergo
when he lay, patient and resigned, awaiting his dismissal
from earth, and, extending towards us his thin, white

hand, said, with much emotion, " I am going to my long home !"

It is impossible that the mind can exclude and shut out, at all times, the memory of the past. How often will the scenes of the year so lately gone by, and those of that upon which we have just entered, be present with us in the future,—even many years hence, should we be permitted to live ! Yes,

> " The memory of the past will come,
> To meet us face to face."

And though the School-band has long been broken, and many of our youthful companions are now scattered over the " wide wide world," and others,—like poor Harry, —are gone to their long home, yet each familiar name is still remembered. And though the light in the *old School-room* has long been extinguished, and he who watched there is now seen no more, yet there are many living to testify to his unpretending worth, his blameless and respected life, his reputable attainments, and lamented death. And a visit to the little sequestered and interesting church-yard of Zennor, or a look at the *old School-room* at St. Just, never fails to revive in the memory the name of JOHN DAVY.— J. W.

HOME.

FAREWELL, my long, my loved abode, farewell !
Where peace, content, and simple manners dwell;
Where rustic scenes in guileless shades appear,
And rural quiet crowns the circling year.
No more may I thy loved domain survey,
Or down thy vale pursue my pensive way ;
No more may I ascend, with cheerful feet,
Thy heath-clad hills, with nature's fragrance sweet.—
The withering blasts of Winter's dreary reign,
That sweep the mountain, devastate the plain,
Fall chastened on thee in that lowly dale,
Securely hid when angry storms prevail.—

That rural village, though unknown to fame,
What memories waken even at the name !
How oft within that hallowed spot, my home,

B

I've passed the lonely hour of midnight gloom

In unremitted labours, thus to store

My youthful mind with scientific lore !

And, when stern Winter ruled with icy sway,

And cares subsided with the closing day,

How oft the villagers would then retire,

To spend the evening round the cheerful fire !

And each, in turn, would some fond theme relate,

Not of perplexing plans to mend the state,

Or seriously renew some oft-told tale,

Or ancient legend of some spectre pale,

Or wondrous deeds by their good fathers done,

And stories strange, long passed, denied by none.

These, oft renewed, afforded, still, delight,

Supplied the theme, and thus beguiled the night.

And though for them no sumptuous boards displayed

Their ample stores, superfluously arrayed,—

Our needless wants by reason are denied,— .

Their own were few, and these their means supplied.

For them no scenes of revelry had power

To cheat the value of each passing hour;

Or midnight mirth that lulls to noontide ease,

So oft debasing while it tends to please :

To manly toil the honest rustics rose,

At early dawn, from nights of sweet repose ;

Their labours, crowned with heaven's approving smile,

Brought health, and peace, and sweet content the while.

Though years have passed, I still delight to trace

The simple scenes of this, my native place ;

The humble cot, the dear sequestered vale,

The rippling brook, whose murmurs never fail ;

Along whose bourn how often have I strayed,

When men and nature in repose were laid ;

In pensive mood the midnight hour beguiled,

Amid those scenes that lured me from a child ;

Heaven's glorious dome surveyed with raptured view;

Nor wished for scenes beyond what then I knew.

Whate'er my lot, where'er my path shall tend,

While on life's pilgrimage my steps I bend ;

B 2

Whatever spot on earth's domain I see,

My memory still will fondly turn to thee ;

To thee 'twill turn. to thee this heart is true,

Where with my youth that cherished friendship grew

Which still survives. and still with it will blend

Undying memories, to life's latest end.

Those days, long passed, of honest youthful prime,

Those many interviews at evening time ;

Those oft-frequented haunts, and pathways rude,

Where other footsteps rarely did intrnde ;

The sweet repose that wrapped the rural scene,

As oped the Sabbath, peaceful and serene ;

And youth, and age, and manly prime were there,

Bending their footsteps to the house of prayer,

While on the ear, in pleasing accents, fell

The soothing echoes of the Sabbath bell :

These loved mementoes memory still reveres,

And will survive amid the waste of years.

Blest is that spot where scenes like these abound!

'Tis doubly hallowed, consecrated ground ;

Where memory fondly lingers, and pourtrays

The stirring incidents of other days,   .

Of days and years whose potent spells, combined,

Enchain, in pleasing retrospect, the mind;

And scenes long passed omnipotently rise,

And wake the bosom's hidden sympathies ;

And memories now, that in repose have lain,

Glow in their native ardour once again.

Dear is that nook of earth, where once we played

In childish innocence, or fondly strayed

In manly prime its pleasing scenes among,

While Nature, vocal with resounding song,

At morn and evening lifted up her voice,

And bade the universe in God rejoice.

   The winding path—my feet may tread no more—

The brook, that rippled near my father's door ;

The grassy sward, where oft I tranquil lay

At evening time, and sighed my cares away;

Friends, yet surviving, or consigned to tears,

The village matron, and the man of years

Whose patriarchal reign, with wisdom crowned,

Demanded reverence from all around :

These all, in glowing, prominent, array,

Seem vivid still, as scenes of yesterday.

But, dearer far than these, than all to me,

Those household gatherings I no more shall see,

As round the board, or round the hearth we came,

A peaceful household, one in hope and aim.

Parental counsel there, with mild behest,

Found ready entrance in each youthful breast ;

And oft the wholesome admonition came,—

" Prize, more than wealth, an honest, virtuous, name;

That, virtue, truth, and industry afford;

Their priceless blessings, on life's chequered road,

Lead to a peaceful, honoured, blest, repose,

When life's tumultuous pilgrimage shall close."

But ah ! those lips that syllabled for me

These wholesome precepts from my infancy,

Their accents now salute my ear no more !

Passed are those days, their artless scenes are o'er !

No more shall I, at evening's tranquil reign,

Meet those beloved ones round that hearth again ;

No more shall I behold each form and face,

Within the precincts of that hallowed place :

Yet, wheresoe'er my pilgrim feet shall roam,

However distant from that humble home,

Each form, each face, and each familiar name,

In memory's record they are still the same ;

And time but hallows the remembrance, dear,

Which stronger grows with each revolving year.

TO A THRUSH.

HAST thou commenced so soon thy matin song,
   Greeting the earliest beams of dewy morn
With thy sweet melodies, that float along
   Upon the fragrant-laden zephyr borne !
And on my listening ear thy warblings fall
   Like the rich strains struck from some harp unseen,
So rapid, clear, and sweet, with scarce a pause between.

And while my anguished heart doth heave with sighs,
   And from my eyes flows down the gushing tear,
To think how many woes beneath the skies
   Hath frail humanity to suffer here,
Thou hast a note of gladness, varied, sweet;
   Like music gushing forth from babbling rills
It comes ! it comes ! my heart with joy and gladness fills.

And oft I'm waking ere the dappled grey

    Of morn is painted in the orient sky,

Waiting to catch thy first rich, thrilling, lay,

    Ere downy slumber seals again my eye ;

And sure as Morn, in robes of silvery light,

    Profusely pours his beams the earth to cheer,

So sure thy warblings come, familiar, sweet, and clear.

Sing on thou innocent and fluttering thing!

    Still pour thy lays upon the breast of morn!

There is enough of discord here to wring

    My anguished heart, that oft with grief is torn;

Fain would I hide where misery never comes,

    And thy sweet minstrelsy might yield repose,

Till discord be no more, or life's brief day shall close.

What joyous melody is thine each morn !

    The perfumed breath of fragrant Summer flowers

Is not more grateful, on the breezes borne,

    Than is the minstrelsy thy voice still pours.

May naught alarm, or mar, thy matin song !

May no rude hand abridge thy little day !
And may thy life but close with thy last thrilling lay!

And, when the mantling robe of eve is thrown,
    In crimson glory, o'er the western main,
In some sweet bower may'st thou then nestle down
    'Neath skies serene, and Summer's tranquil reign!
Where teaming wild flowers shed their rich perfume,
    Where murmuring rills and evening zephyrs play,
To blend in sweet accord with thy last thrilling lay.

THE SABBATH.

WRITTEN IN THE COUNTRY.

HAIL ! holy Sabbath, day of rest,
  Oh! what enchantment in the sound !
The day, above all others, blest,
  With thousand, thousand, mercies crowned.

The air is fragrant, soft, and clear :
  No sound is borne upon the breeze,
To mar the calm, or meet the ear,
  Save song of bird, or hum of bees.

The din of rural life is still,
  The villagers from labour cease ;
Along the vale, and up the hill,
  The cattle seem to browse in peace.

All Nature, now, reposing lies,
 As if to greet this hallowed morn ;
And wide her rich oblations rise
 To heaven, upon the breeze upborne.

The city's din is hushed this day,
 And, lo! her towers and temples rise ;
They seem to prompt her tribes to pay
 Their vows and homage to the skies.

Each Sabbath morn, the knell, how sweet !
 That charms the ear, and soothes the breast,
That calls us forth, with cheerful feet,
 To raise to heaven the warm request.

It sounds o'er moorland, hill, and dale,
 O'er haunts where late the masses trod ;
And, as it floats upon the gale,
 It seems as 'twere a voice from God.

Britannia's cannons' awful roar
 Spreads terror, wide as pole from pole ;

But, oh ! her Sabbath chimes steal o'er,
   And thrill with melody, the soul.

Her homes where rural joys abide,
   See ! youth and age from thence retire :—
The maiden in her modest pride,
   The matron in her neat attire.

With cheerful step, and reverent air,
   They tread the temple's awful space :
And manhood, youth, and age are there.
   And voices blend in prayer and praise.

But not alone in gothic aisles
   Is worship paid to God most high,
In noble consecrated piles,
   That lift their towers to meet the sky.

Where'er the humblest house for prayer,
   The contrite heart, the suppliant voice,
God is pre-eminently there,
   To bid that contrite heart rejoice

Till time its rapid course shall still,

   Or Britain's name shall cease to be,

Still may her tribes her temples fill!

   Our Island's pride from sea to sea.

LITTLE CHILDREN.

AN INCIDENT.

LITTLE children! on the lea,
Laughing, now, at sight of me,
Wondering wherefore I appear
One among your number here:—
Though no talk has taken place
I can read it in your face ;
Ay ! I guess, while you I see,
Such are now your thoughts of me.—
Well, my little children ! I,
Gladly now, will tell you why
I am come to look at you,
And to share your pleasures too,
At this quiet evening hour,
Fragrant with the hawthorn's flower :

By the murmuring, crystal ri.

While the dew is falling, still ;

You, I come with joy to greet,

Little rose-buds at my feet,

Opening into life each hour,

Fresher, fairer, than the flower ;

Lambkins in Creation's fold,

Fairest gems of earthly mould

Miniatures of manhood, ye!

Man in all his majesty.

Not the stars, that beam so bright,

Burning in the brow of night ;

Not the rubies, rich and rare,

Which the monarch's crown doth bear ;

Nor the flowers that deck the vale,

Nodding to the gentle gale,

Crystalled o'er with drops of dew,

Look so beautiful as you.

On those dimpled checks so fair,

Oh ! what innocence is there !

In the beaming of those eyes,
What unuttered language lies !
And those accents, soft and clear,
Angels now might list to hear :
Oh! that ever you should be
Scathed by sin, or misery !
I have come, from noise away,
Not to scare you from your play,
Come, and as, by chance, we meet
In this flowery nook, so sweet,
Let your little sports abound !
Crop the beauteous flowers around !
Blue-eyed violets near the rill,
Gather these, and prattle still !
And let me be one with you,
See your bliss, and share it too :
Let me here with you remain ;
Let me be a child again.
Scowl, thou stern philosophy !
I would not be linked to thee :

C

Here thou shalt not now intrude

With thy precepts, stern and crude ;

Oft our bliss we make, or find,

From the temper of the mind ;

True philosophy is this,

In the present find your bliss.

Let him scowl who will at me,

Linked again to infancy,

Him, who never, since his birth,

Beauty saw, in heaven or earth;

He shall not abridge my bliss,

In a fairy realm like this.

Here, again, I can review

Childhood's happy hours, anew,

Paint the fields, the flowers, so fair,

And the faces that were there;

Can, in memory's mirror, trace

Each endeared and hallowed place;

Where the daisies covered o'er

Sloping mead and level moor,

And the whole, before my eyes,

Like a fairy region lies.

Children! now my heart is full,

While I see the flowers you cull;

Types of you, in bloom arrayed,

Oh! too soon, perhaps, to fade ;

Or, like stars, at opening day,

Melting in the light away ;

Or as pearly dews, that gleam

In the sun's resplendent beam,

Soon, exhalèd,—disappear,

Wafted to a higher sphere ;

Thus, how oft your life appears

Ushered in, then closed in tears !

Words I have not to reveal

All that in my heart I feel.

I have wept for children, too,

Fair and beautiful as you ;

Seen them fade in health and bloom,

c 2

Laid them in an early tomb ;

Watched the little heaving breast,

Till, at last, it sank to rest ;

Marked the hectic cheek inflame,

When convulsion shook the frame.

Then, I prayed, oppressed with grief,

" Let this agony be brief !

End, O God! these mortal throes !

Let this life of suffering close!

Take the spirit home to thee,

God of awful majesty!"

Children! I must now forbear,

And the parting hour is near.

Nor ought I to cloud your mood,

Mar your bliss, or here intrude

With a plaintive tale, that may

Banish cheerfulness away.

Fare ye well, in life and death,

Sojourners upon this earth !

You will meet, and have to brave,

Many a tempest-threatening wave.

Fare ye well, when storms shall lower,

When shall come the darkest hour ;

Blest and prosperous may you be,

Over life's tempestuous sea !

Find a haven from the blast

In the heavenly home, at last !

WHAT IS THE GOAL THOU HAST
IN VIEW ?

WHAT is the goal thou hast in view ?
  In life's career what is thy aim ?
Is it to dare some noble deed,
  With which to blend a deathless name ?
Is it the lofty realm to reach
  Of intellectual thought sublime,
The altitude from whence thy fame
  Shall travel down to future time ?

God speed thee in this noble aim,
  This dignified design, that may
Immortalize thy name ; but, know
  To this there is a toilsome way ;
A rugged uphill path to climb,
  To test thy energies and skill ;

Thy soul's best attributes to try,
    Thy firm resolve and noblest will.

The hand that never casts the seed
    Within the furrows of the soil,
At length may reap, and often does,
    The harvest of another's toil :
Not so with thee, in fields of lore :
    If thou the golden grain would'st see,
And reap deserved renown at length,
    Thy toil must unremitted be.

Art thou a man with life oppressed,
    And doomed to toil the live-long day ?
To earn with sweated brow thy bread ?
    Cast not thy fortitude away.
My fellow! nobly dare thy part
    In life's career, and know that thou
Art dignified by honest toil,
    And bear'st the impress on thy brow.

In God's own image thou wert made;
 Thy manly form, thy noble mould,
Still bears the fashion of His hand,
 Thine origin sublime of old ;
And He thine earthly bounds hath set,
 Thy task in life He hath assigned ;
Fulfil it bravely, as a man
 Of stern resolve and noble mind.

Nor yield thy spirit to despair;
 A magnanimity acquire
To stem the roughest tide of life,
 To nerve thee in the fiercest fire;
And deeply in thy heart be laid
 An inwrought power, a faith to say
That yet the Providence of God
 Will turn the darkest night to day.

But, oh ! perhaps, thy hearth has been
 Bereft of those, beloved of old,
And thou art stricken down with grief

That such no more thou dost behold ;
A change hath passed o'er all within
　　The precincts of home's hallowed sphere,
And sighs are heaved, and tears are shed,
　　For those that are no longer there.

Well, call to mind, and let the thought
　　Compose, sustain, and yield relief,
That He who made thee what thou art,
　　Who bruised thee, will assuage thy grief ;
And know, there is a moral power,
　　A true philosophy of mind,
To man thee 'gainst the ruthless blast,
　　Thy heart amid the storm to bind.

The chastened heart will oft endure
　　An anguish man might shrink to name ;
Nor cans't thou, while untried, define
　　Its strength to bear the testing flame;
And, in the midnight of thy woe,
　　While yet thy spirit prostrate lies,

All blasted, lo! the morning ray
   Is nearing now, to greet thine eyes.

The wilderness, all parched and dry,
   The smitten rock, the manna given,
The olive leaf of Noah's dove,
   The bow that spanned the vault of heaven ;
The morn, in clouds and tempest wrapped,
   The evening, calm, serene, and clear ;
Remember these, and dare to hope
   A brighter day will soon appear.

ON THE DEATH OF A SISTER.

NO idle theme in fancy's mirror wrought,
No vain, illusive, and fictitious thought,
Shall prompt me now, or nerve my hand to write,
Or fan the flame that would to verse incite,
Or sway my breast, that sorrow's pang hath proved
For thee, my sister, from this world removed :
But all my numbers shall with truth agree
To sketch thy portraiture, so dear to me.

Though I may joy thy virtues to rehearse,
I mourn for thee, the subject of my verse ;
For thee, descended to the grave full soon—
Ere thine ascending sun had reached his noon.
I mourn that now thy voice no more I hear,
Breaking melodious on my listening ear ;—
Yet may I joy that, on the heavenly plains,
That voice resounds in more exalted strains !

How oft, when evening's tranquil reign began,
Domestic bliss through all the circle ran,
As round the fireside, still in memory sweet,
We then were wont, with mutual joy, to meet,
To pass the hour in music's sweet employ,
And all the luxury of home enjoy!
How oft thy voice then o'er my spirit stole,
And thrilled with ecstacy my inmost soul!

And though thy seat beside that peaceful hearth,
Where thy loved presence gave our pleasures birth,
Is vacant now, and thou no more art found
One of the family who that hearth surround;
Yet near the eternal throne thou sitt'st among
That ransomed and innumerable throng
Whose robes are washed in the all-cleansing blood
Of Christ, the spotless, bleeding Lamb of God.
Thy wasted form by days of suffering here,
Thy nights of anguish, ah! those pains severe!
Thine eyes undimmed that beamed so calm in death,

Thy christian triumph with thy latest breath,

Thy voice, thy smile, thy looks, thy words, so kind,

And every virtue that adorned thy mind,

In memory's record they are still the same,

As when in life my lips pronounced thy name.

Sister, farewell! thou now from earth art free,

And from the sorrows which encompass me ;

The ills of life, that o'er my pathway roll,

Shall never more disturb thy tranquil soul ;

But if 'tis ours on earth to realize

The ministry of angels from the skies,

And guardian saints around our pathway meet,

To save from circling snares our pilgrim feet ;

May thy blest shade my watchful guardian be,

When hidden snares and sorrows compass me ;

When lowering clouds upon my path descend,

And gathering storms and thickest darkness blend,

To blast my hopes, my fortitude destroy,

And quite annihilate my rising joy!

Oh ! be thou near, thou spirit of the blest,
And hush to calm the tempest of my breast!—
Point me to realms where joys perpetual rise,
And lure my burthened spirit to the skies!

If grief can move, or melt, a mother's breast,
Just on the verge of heaven's eternal rest,
'Tis when resigning to a world of cares
Her helpless infant, child of many prayers ;
That grief was thine, when she, in whom I trace
Thyself, was folded in thy last embrace ;
For her thy prayer in fervent accents rose,
Preferred with all a dying mother's throes;
And still with glowing, yet affections mild,
Perhaps thy spirit hovers o'er thy child ;
Watches each step when unseen ills are near,
Knows every sigh, and numbers every tear ;
Delights to see—thy bliss enhanced the while—
The self-same actions, still endearing smile,
And pleased to hear her lisp a Saviour's name,

In prayers which thou did'st teach her lips to frame.

Thy strength, thy ardour, of maternal love

Nor time, nor change, nor place, can e'er remove,

But shall exist when years have rolled away,

Till the last tint of life's protracted day

Shall fade, expire, and, on her opening sight,

Bursts the full blaze of heaven's eternal light;

And thou, and thine, again shall meet, and be

From storm and tempest, earth and suffering free.

SPRING IS COMING !

SPRING is coming!   Yes, the fragrance
  Of the primrose scents the breeze;
Ushered in by feathered songsters,
  Opening flowers, and budding trees.
Spring is coming ! o'er the meadows
  See! the sportive lambkins bound,
While the beauteous blue-eyed violets,
  And the daisies, stud the ground.

Spring is coming!   Long and dreary
  Hath been Winter's ruthless reign,
With its devastating tempests
  Sweeping over land and main;
Hearts and homes are filled with anguish,
  Where there late was joy and mirth:

And the widow, with her orphans,
   Weep around the lonely hearth ;

Weep, alas ! for those departed,
   Loved ones, lost ones, now asleep
Where kind hands will never wake them,
   In the chambers of the deep ;
Raging wars, and fearful tempests,
   Deaths and famines, all have been
Since the gentle Spring was with us,
   Robing earth in living green.

Long and anxious have we waited
   For the vivifying Spring,
Waking into life and beauty
   Nature with its pencilling ;
Up the mountains while we wander,
   Through the valley, o'er the mead,
Twice ten thousand flowers are springing,
   All in beauty, 'neath our tread.

D

Spring is coming ! Let us greet it,
 While, with gladness and delight,
We behold the pictured landscape
 Spread before the joyous sight ;
See the verdant mead bespangled
 With the crystal drops of dew ;—
In those atoms of creation
 There are worlds that meet the view.—

Spring is coming ! Nature owns it,
 And, responsive, she is seen
Waking from her Wintry slumber,
 Swathed in habiture of green ;
With the hues of health and beauty
 Broadly o'er her features cast ;
Lo ! to life she is returning,
 Now the reign of death is past.

And the radiant sun, enshrouded
 Late and long,—in darkness drowned,—
Now is shedding his effulgence,

Life and light, on all around ;
And the flower-bespangled meadow,
    Mountain, moorland, grove, and glen,
'Neath his genial influence waken
    Into beauty once again.

Spring is coming ! Morn and evening,
    Singing birds, and opening flowers,
All proclaim it ; lo ! 'tis with us,
    Brighter suns will soon be ours.
Yes ! the odour-laden zephyr,—
    Summer's grateful, fragant, sigh,—
With the affluence of flowers,
    Soon our earth will beautify.

SUGGESTED BY A VIEW

FROM CAPE CORNWALL, IN 1830.

THE toils of the day with the peasant were ending,
And homeward the rustic was bent on his way ;
Aloft was the incense of evening ascending ;
And briskly around were the lambkins at play.

The breeze and the billow their murmurs were blending ;
The sun in his glory was hastening down;
On the crystal abyss was his radiance extending ;
And grandeur the reign of the evening did crown.

The ponderous rocks overhanging the ocean,
The echoes that rise from the neighbouring strand,
The barque on the waters, the birds in commotion,
The burst of the billow so awfully grand,

Conspire to strike and command the attention,

 And fill with a nameless emotion the soul,

An emotion that sways it without a declension,

 As the billows beneath one in majesty roll.

And, far, far, away, from the din of confusion.

 Where naught inharmonious was borne on the breeze,

How mean, I bethought, were the haunts of intrusion !

 Compared with my prospect, how seldom they please !

And there seemed in the stir of the waters so pleasant,

 And gentlest zephyr that played on the flood,

The omnific voice of a Deity present;

 And all things around bore the impress of God.

TO MY CHILD ASLEEP.

MY boy ! so cherub-like, and sweet,
    Unconscious of the cares and fears
That wait the progress of thy feet,
    A pilgrim in this world of tears :

An heir to all the ills between
    The cradle and the oblivious grave ;
Thy heritage a troubled scene,
    Embarked on life's tempestuous wave.

Ah ! yes, that tranquil breast and form,
    With angel innocence o'ercast,
That breast must soon feel sorrow's storm ;
    The flight of years that form must blast.

Then sleep, my boy ! nor wake too soon,
　　Life's opening morning now is thine ;
Those golden hours ere sultry noon,
　　And cares that press on life's decline.

May calm repose prolong, sweet one,
　　Those smiles that o'er thy features play,
Bespeaking sympathies unknown,
　　Of spirit with the mortal clay.

Wherefore those smiles ?—perhaps this hour,
　　Commissioned from the spheres divine,
Some guardian spirit watches o'er,
　　And holds communion now with thine.

What hopes and fears alternate sway
　　My bosom while I gaze on thee,
And contemplate thy future day
　　Of happiness, or misery!

Now fear pourtrays the storms that lower,
　　To blast the fairest form of clay ;
And life appears a fleeting hour,
　　At best a chequered Winter's day.

And now, what joys within me rise,
　　As hope the cheering scene pourtrays,
And, mirrored in her ambient skies,
　　I see the bliss of future days !

I trust, my boy ! when ripening years
　　Shall stamp thy brow with manly mien,
No rising grief, or falling tears,
　　Will mark my life at thought of thine.

But, blest in thee, whom wisdom's voice,
　　Shall lure to tread the path of joy ;
Through life this heart will oft rejoice
　　O'er thee, my sweet unconscious boy.

And, when thou on the stream of time
   Shalt, soon or later, near the grave,
May steadfast faith, and hope sublime.
   Sustain in death's tempestuous wave!

These shall support thy sinking head,
   As, weary, thou shalt yield thy breath,
And point to realms beyond the dead,
   Where dwells not grief, nor pain, nor death.

THE MISSIONARY.

HE is gone from his home, and the land of his birth,
And the peaceful retreat of his own sweet hearth,
And the smiles that around his childhood played,
And the forms that now in the dust are laid :
But in memory's view they are still the same,
And thrill to his soul with a quenchless flame.

He is gone from that home of his earliest breath,
To the scene of his labours, of dangers and death,
Whence the piteous cries the degraded to save
Were borne on the breeze as he crossed on the wave;
To the land where the sweet Sabbath dawn ne'er smiled,
To the land with the rites of the heathen defiled.

He is gone where the mother, well pleased, hath stood,

With her hands imbrued in her infant's blood ;

Where the flames arose with her dying groans

As she was consumed with her husband's bones ;

And shouts were loud from those who came

To gaze on the all-devouring flame.

He is gone where death and diseases waste,

As the scorching sun, or the withering blast ;

And the scattered bones of the pilgrim, old,

Are white on the desert sands, and cold :

And savage hoards, with the murderous steel,

Are fierce as the noontide heats they feel.

He is gone where the rills of crystal stray,

And the rustling woods in the breezes play,

And the skies are calm o'er sunny lands,

And the seas are girt with golden sands,

And nature wears her loveliest suit;

But man is depraved as the forest brute.

He is gone to exalt from the depths of the fall, _
For the cries of the heathen have entered his soul :
And lo ! as the banner is raised on high,
And the cross, with its marks of agony,
The darkness of ages is scattered wide !
As the mist that rolls from the mountain's side.

And the isles of the sea, with their tribes untold,
And the heathenish wastes, with their idols of old,
Have witnessed his toil, and weariless zeal,
Till. alas ! in the noon of his labours he fell,
A victim devoted to death, to save
From that which impended beyond the grave.

Though he sleeps not now in the land of his birth,
With his fathers, who slumber beneath the green earth,
Yet the palm tree spreads its peaceful shade
O'er the sacred spot where his bones are laid ;
And his spirit hath soared to the realms of light,
For ever to dwell in his Maker's sight.

A BIRTHDAY SUGGESTION FOR A LADY.

HOW fragrant and fair is the opening rose !
  ·Regaling at noontide, at evening, and morn :
'Tis an emblem of life as its beauties disclose ;
   'Tis an emblem of life when its beauties are shorn.

In Spring there's the bud of its future array,
  In Summer it blooms in its richest attire,
Ere Winter it fades and dies swiftly away ;
   Yes ! swiftly its fragrance and glory expire.

And such is our life as it fleets along fast,
  And year after year steals the vigour it gave ;
The Spring and the Summer are hastily passed,
   And the Winter is closed in the gloom of the grave.

The forest, all mantled in foliage so green,
　　And kissed by the breath of the Summer benign,
Disrobed by the blasts of the Autumn is seen :
　　An emblem of life in its youth and decline.

And all things around us are changing, and naught
　　Of this world is to us now as once it was seen ;
Each period, receding for ever, is fraught
　　With hopes that are kindled, or blighted have been.

But the gem that adorns and ennobles your youth,
　　And crowns the meridian of life with a grace,
Is found in the ways of religion and truth,
　　Nor shall Death, with his terrors, its beauties efface.

MIDNIGHT REFLECTIONS.

THE sun hath sunk beneath the western hills,

And 'round me now are closed the shades of night,

Which wrap in darkness, solemn and profound,

Valley and plain, and mountain towering high,

With all the complicated works of man.

Then, may this hour of darkness, deep and still,

And thou dread Spirit of eternal truth,

Awake to thoughtfulness my careless soul !

Bid me contemplate one profound display

Of God's Almighty hand, which hung on high

Those rolling globes of light, unnumbered worlds,

Which unto man, in silent language, prove

Some great first cause : those rolling spheres on high,

And the deep stillness of this awful hour,

Stirring the inmost soul with thoughts that swell,

And fain would find an utterance in words ;

But speech is lost, and man is awed and dumb
In presence of his Maker and His works ;
And silent adoration best befits
Where all is awful, deep, sublime, and still.

No! not a sound is heard, save of the ripple
Of yon small stream, that wanders down the vale,
In murmurs soft, or distant rumbling of
The ocean wave, that ceases not to heave.
The noontide gale hath gently died away ;
The feathered songsters of the leafy grove,
With whose melodious and delightful strains
The valleys lately rang, have sunk to rest.
The busy hum of industry hath ceased ;
The sounds that commerce poured upon the breeze
Are heard no more, but with the breeze expired.
Man, too, hath ceased to prosecute the day,
Whose toilsome hours exhaust his hardy strength,
And on his couch reclined his weary frame
Fast fallen in the arms of balmy sleep ; —

Sleep, emblematic of the night of death,

When the long, toilsome, day of life shall close,

And man lies down fatigued, not soon to wake,

Or rise at early dawn, with strength renewed,

To scour, with active step, the upland height,

Or reap the fruitful field, or fell the wood,

Or round the social hearth to sit, elate

With the sweet prattling of his offspring gay,

But in the grave reposes, till shall come

The final hour of death's unbroken sleep,

And he shall wake, an endless course pursue,

Eternity's unbroken, boundless, day.

What is that state? its secrets, who can name?

How anxiously the spirit tries to sound

Its deep and fathomless abyss! to know

Its hidden mysteries! What thoughts arise

Within me as I dwell upon the vast,

And never yet explored, expanse beyond!

Fain would the soul, that ever pants to know

The future, try to uplift the veil and look

E

Into the world beyond, that spirit land,

Flooded with light, unseen by mortal eye.

   Will there the woes of earth to me be known ?—

The widow's sighing, and the orphan's tears ?

The tyrant's reign, the despot's cruel sway ?

The broken hearted, and down-stricken, ones.

Whom the oppressor mercilessly crushed ?

Will there the scenes of earth my thoughts engage ?

Its weal or woe ? Or will the range of vast

Eternity to come so open up

Its all-absorbing truths, awful, sublime,

That my immortal vision shall remain

For ever fixed in steadfast gaze thereon,

And earth, and earthly scenes, engage no more?

   What thoughts crowd on me at this solemn hour !—

The world that is, and that which is to come ;

Time, and eternity ; immortal life ;

My future being ; what that being is,

And how sustained. What shall I know, or be ;

Or what behold ? What is a spirit ? Where

Are now the myriads that have passed away ?

I feel the stirrings of a deathless soul,

That fain these mysteries would understand :

But, no! it cannot be, till I have put

This mortal off, and passed the bounds of time.

Oh ! how confounding is the link that binds

The flesh and spirit ! What disclosures new,

Awful and great, are pending on what seem

So simple, yet so marvellous and grand !

Let but the life-blood of my heart be stilled ;

The pulse, and labouring breast, but cease to heave ;

The mortal vision be but closed in death,

And then, the revelation comes ! the veil

Is put aside ! the mist dispelled ! and bursts

The dazzling light of vast eternity,

All instantaneous, on the spirit, just

With wonder launched upon the deep abyss !

And, what I know not now, I then shall know,

   So fearfully and wonderfully made

   E 2

Am I, myself I cannot understand;
And am confounded when I but reflect
On what I am. The ever active mind,
That can, at will, dwell on the ages yet
To come, can, in an instant, also scan
The scenes and incidents long since transpired;
And at this solemn hour, when all is still,
How vividly I see the past! it comes
All fresh to memory, like the daylight scenes
That passed but yesterday before my sight.
The school companions, and the school boy feats;
Our old preceptor, hale at eighty years,
Of form so huge, and of such reverend mien,
That my young heart would palpitate with fear,
Whene'er his anger and his frown awoke.
Methinks I see him now, hoary with age,
Yet with an eye so piercing that, whene'er
His ire was kindled,—as it often was,
Alas! too justly, at our heedless ways,—
His look at once rebuke effectual gave.

To note our progress, oft the vicar came ;

A man of much benevolence of face,

And nature too; his aim—to live in peace,

And harmony, with all. And often, while

The last sad, solemn, service for the dead

He did perform, around we stood ; and, when

The mourners lifted up their voice and wept,

My youthful breast was oft surcharged with grief

To see the dreary grave closed darkly o'er

The late departed one, so much deplored.

And now the appointed time, by him prefixed,

Arrives for us to stand around him in

The venerable aisle ; where he was wont

To question us in what he, doubtless, deemed

Duty to God and man. No irksome task

Was ours, but cheerfully fulfilled ; for he

Was ever wont to pass our failings by,

Nor harshly censure where a fault he saw.

Strange that such incidents as these should now

In retrospect arise ! but thus it is ;

And memory paints them all in fresh array.

The churchyard, which, in grave and solemn mood,

I many a time since then have loitered o'er,

Was oft the play-ground : there, at noon, and eve,

Each was ambitious to surpass the rest,

The highest grave-stone to surmount; how yet

Familiar is the one I've often tried,

But unsuccessful ! I a junior was,

And this was wide and high.   All is, indeed,

Familiar yet:—the Christmas morning bells ;

Anthems and carols at the service time;

The silvery-headed sires, who duly trod,

On Sabbath days, the precincts of God's house ;

The better folk ; the rustics, ranged around ;

The pillared, sacred, venerable, aisles,

Which oft re-echoed with such beauteous strains

That I have heard of aged men to tears

Melted, as rose the sacred, solemn, swell

Of music from rich voices, all attuned

In noble and harmonious concert joined.

ON THE EMANCIPATION OF THE SLAVES

IN THE WEST INDIES, IN 1834.

HARK! upon the ear it throngs,
  Cheering as the light of day,
Louder than ten thousand tongues,
  Sweeter than the virgin's lay.

'Tis the voice that freedom pours,
  Thrilling through the abject soul,
Nursed in Eden's hallowed bowers;
  Let it spread from pole to pole!

Britain! nobler, dearer, grown
  By the ransom thou hast paid,
By those miseries, not thine own,
  Which thy generous hand hath stayed:

In thy senatorial voice,

    England! still of matchless fame,

Thousands, thousands, now rejoice,

    Thousands, thousands, bless thy name.

Now are heard, across the wave,

    Shouts, thy recent laws inspire,,

Where the poor, the abject, slave

    Bled beneath the tyrant's ire :

See him there!—my fellow man,

    Bent beneath his iron frown;

Through his veins what transport ran,

    As he flung his shackles down !

See his soul imbued with fire,

    Deathless as my own to be ;

Ah! it throbs with strong desire,

    Swells and throbs for liberty.

In that soul's convulsive sighs
  Bruised and agonized with grief,
There's a voice to God that cries,
  Cries for justice and relief.

God, Almighty ! from Thy throne,
  Interpose, redress, release !
Yes! where'er a slave is known,
  Bid his wrongs for ever cease !

Is he not my fellow ?—nay,
  One in essence, name, and mould ?
Wherefore, in the light of day,
  Is he shackled, bought, and sold ?

Oh ! repress the monster ill,
  Foulest blot on manhood's name :
Am I not a man, to feel
  This is my reproach and shame ?

Nature, with repugnance brave,
　　Stands abashed at, loathes the sound
Of, a fellow man a slave,
　　Prostrate, helpless, bleeding, bound.

Slavery ! be that name accursed ;
　　Yes ! from every human tongue
Let the execration burst,
　　Till its knell on earth be rung !

Till erect beneath the sky,
　　And his claims acknowledged be,
Every slave shall stand, and cry,
　　" I for evermore am free !"

Freedom,—reason's quenchless light,
　　Nature's loud instinctive call ;—
'Tis the omnipotence of right,
　　God's primeval gift to all.

'Tis the soul's uplifted cry,
  Breathed by man in every clime,
Rising ceaseless to the sky,
  Loud, impassioned, and sublime.

When the heavens shall flee away,
  And the fate of earth is sealed,—
In that last tremendous day,
  When all secrets are revealed;

What unuttered wrongs and woes,
  Africa! so long oppressed,
Will that judgment-day disclose,
  Which have wrung thy bleeding breast !—

Since thy bruised and broken heart,
  Bared to God's all-seeing eye,
Throbbed with sorrow, felt the smart,
  Heaved the agonizing sigh ;

Since the tears that first were wrung
    From thy slaved, degraded, race,
When was wrenched the babe who clung
    To its mother's last embrace.

Say, what tears since then have run,
    And what hearts since then have bled :
Oh! 'twould break a heart of stone,
    Slavery's victims, slaughtered, dead.

Say, ye ocean waves! that lave
    Afric's broad and burning sands,
Say, how many a shackled slave
    Ye have borne to other lands!

What the human forms ye bore
    Far away, enslaved, and sold;
To return, alas! no more ;
    Bartered for the lust of gold !

And, ye groves, and glens, and plains,
    Haunts where nature's children strayed,
Where eternal summer reigns
    In the forest's deepest shade ;

Say, what tears have steeped your soil,
    And what hearts in ruin lain,
Since the monster came to spoil,
    And bear off, your tribes, for gain!

Not the sun's meridian rays,
    Vertical, to scorch the ground,
Falling with untempered blaze,
    Stunting nature all around ;

Nor the fearful lightning-fire,
    Nor the blast that sweeps the plain,
Ever spread such ruin dire
    As vile slavery's cursèd reign.

What a long and woeful night,
   Africa ! hath closed thee round !
When shall break the morning light,
   To dispel thy gloom profound ?

When shall burst the glorious day ?
   When shall slavery's reign be o'er ?
And its miseries pass away,
   To be known on earth no more ?

Is it yours, ye worthies ! say,
   Spirits now in endless light,
To descry this glorious day,
   Bursting from the womb of night ?—

Ye, whose eloquence, of old,
   Grew impassioned with your years ;
In the senate-house it rolled,
   Till the heart dissolved in tears.

Champions, there, ye nobly rose,
  Friends of freedom, and the slave ;
Pleading long, and late, his cause,
  Stretching out the hand to save.

Light, from heaven's eternal throne,
  Radiant in your bosoms glowed,
Undiminished still it shone,
  On, resistless, still it flowed.

And compassion's noble aim,
  Mercy's broad and boundless span,
Kindled in your souls a flame,
  Roused your sympathies for man.

Yes ! for man, degraded, slave,
  Remnant of a wretched race:
And ye nobly aimed to save
  Manhood from this foul disgrace.

Honoured to life's latest end,
    Ages shall augment your fame;—
Ye who nobly sought to blend
    Liberty with manhood's name.

As the sun's resplendent rays,
    Crimsoning the glorious west,
Broader grandeur still displays,
    As he nobly sinks to rest:

Thus your deeds have gained renown,
    Which shall echo through all time,
Thus your earthly sun went down,
    Broad, majestic, and sublime.

TO THE PRIMROSE.

(AN INCIDENT.)

WELCOME! floweret of the Spring,
　With thy soft and modest mien;
Pleasant memories thou dost bring,
　Memories of those days serene
When my childhood oped as free,
And as fresh and fair, as thee.

Here thou art!—a precious gem,—
　And I view thee with delight,
Lovely, fragrant, diadem,
　Richly waving in my sight;
With thy kindred clustering near,
Early flowerets of the year.

See! where now that lady stands;
　Anxiously she looks, the while,

F

With her white extended hands,
  On her countenance a smile :
She is grasping thee with pride,
And thy sisters by thy side.

Might I not here moralize
  On what thou and thine will be,
And on her whose beauteous eyes
  Longingly are cast on thee;
When your forms, so graceful, must
Fade, and mingle with the dust ?

Yes! that form and face, so fair,
  Turned so placidly on thee,
Like a flower in desert air,
  Ah ! too soon must stricken be :
Both must wither 'neath the blast,
Ere its ravages be past.

Fair, but fleeting, things ye are:
  Seen in sunshine and in shade,

Flowers and human life appear,
  Just to flourish, then to fade :
Yet shall both revive, once more,
When death's Wintry reign is o'er.

Thou dids't sleep secure when dread
  Wintry hurricanes were high,
Dareds't not to uplift thy head,
  Nor to ope thy beauteous eye;
But, when early Spring was green,
Thou dids't beautify the scene.

Joying in her primrose prize,
  With elastic, airy, tread,
See ! that gentle lady hies
  On her path across the mead;
With the wreath her home to grace,
Pleasure beaming in her face.

There she will adjust her prize,
  Tending it with fondest care:

F 2

'Neath her mildly-glancing eyes
　　Opening flowers more beauteous are,
As the pearly dewdrops gleam
In the sun's resplendent beam.

In the vase her treasure stands,
　　Every eye it doth allure;
Watered by her gracious hands,
　　Thus a while it shall endure ;—
Emblem of herself most meet,
Blooming, beautiful, and sweet.

But thou never art so fair
　　As when, on thy parent stem,
Thou art waving free as air,
　　Drinking in the noontide beam ;
Then the hedges, lane, and lea,
All are beautified by thee.

Thou art lovely in the shade,
　　And, when in the sunlight found,

Like a blushing, beauteous, maid,
   With thy sisterhood around ;
Soft and modest, sweet and fair,
Even as drooping lilies are.

Earth is lovelier for thee ;
   In thy looks a language lies,
To the ear of poesy
   Speaking of serener skies,
And a myriad fragrant flowers
Basking in the Summer hours.

In what region of the earth
   Dids't thou first in daylight smile ?
Art thou of exotic birth,
   Or did'st spring from Britain's isle ?
On thee did the solar sheen
Flash in Eden's sweet demesne ?

When to Heaven there did ascend
   The first breath of opening flowers,

Did thine incense with it blend,
    Rising up from Eden's bowers ?
Or 'neath skies less fair than those
Did thy beauties first disclose ?

Lovely flower! all hail to thee !
    Gem of Britain's favoured isle,
Blossoming from sea to sea,
    Decking nature with thy smile ;
Thou wilt wake, where'er we roam,
Thoughts, and memories, of home.

Yes ! thou art an English flower ;
    And the traveller, wandering wide,
Pictures every nook and bower,
    And his cottage-home beside,
When, in infancy, he played
In the primrose-sprinkled glade.

Thou dost come to greet our eyes
    When the Winter is no more ;

Cheering as the stars that rise
   When black midnight's reign is o'er ;
Flashing on the joyous sight
Like a radiant beam of light.

While those stars, in vast array,
   Shining since Creation's birth,
God's omnipotence display,
   So the flowers that stud the earth,—
—Starlit heaven, and flowery sod,—
Show the handy-work of God.

ON THE DEATH OF MR. JOHN DAVY,

AN EMINENT MATHEMATICIAN.

COME, pensive muse ! and frame some moving lay,
  On sorrow's harp the plaintive chords prolong ;   .
In artless numbers now the tribute pay
  To him, the subject of thy mournful song.

Friendship, the while, shall heave the genuine sigh,
  To think how death has wrecked the mortal clay
Of him whose soul in Science mounted high,
  Beyond the precincts of inglorious day.

Nobly he soared her Alpine heights among,
  With eye sagacious scanned her wealthy clime ;
Drank of the streams that flow her realms along,
  Till doomed to fall by all-destroying time.

Oh ! death, relentless, 'neath whose ruthless sway
    The sons of science, as the ignoble, fall,
What skill can turn thy pointed shafts away ?
    Or from thy grasp the dearest friend recall?

Ah ! none : the grave enwraps its kindred clay,
    And Davy sleeps within its cold embrace ;
While gathering friends their mournful requiem pay :
    What tears are falling round his resting place !

And though no pomp, nor proud display, be nigh,—
    Too oft in mockery of the unconscious dead,—
No sculptured stone, to strike the enquiring eye
    And mark the spot where rests his hoary head :

Yet worth like thine a noble niche doth claim
    In bosoms warm with friendship's hallowed fire ;
And, in the records of ennobling fame,
    Shall live when pomp and pageantry expire.

Methinks I see that undissembling smile,
   Which gave thy countenance its native grace ;
And hear thy converse flowing on the while,
   And, pleased, the scenes of by-gone years retrace.

But, ah ! those scenes, those years, so soon are past,
   So brief the span where all our bliss doth lie ;
Our joys scarce ripen ere some gathering blast
   Proclaims the end of frendship's pleasures nigh.

And soon must he who now essays to pay
   To thy loved shade this tributary wreath,
Pass, like thyself, from scenes of earth away,
   And quiet rest the mouldering sod beneath.

But there remains,—and may the thought sustain,
   And soothe our spirits 'mid the storms that rise !—
A state where friends unbroken bliss attain,
   And death no conquest, no dominion, tries.

'TIS SUMMER-TIME!

'TIS Summer-time ! 'tis Summer-time !
 And, while beneath these spreading trees
I sit me down, a voice sublime
 I hear upon each gentle breeze ;
It comes from out the verdant sod,
 Enamelled o'er with gems so sweet ;
And syllables the name of God
 In flowers that spring beneath my feet.

I hear it in the murmuring rill,
 Meandering through the leafy shade,
Rich, liquid, gushing, tones, that fill
 With harmony the winding glade :
And on the breath of fragrant flowers
 'Tis borne, surpassing sweet, along ;

From all above, beneath, it pours :
   'Tis nature's universal song.

The fields are dressed in living green,
   The trees their leafy robes unfold,
And God's omnipotence is seen,
   August and glorious to behold ;
The tender blade, the tuneful grove,
   The sun-lit noon, the twilight dim,
The songsters through the air that rove,
   Have all an utterance for Him.

'Tis Summer-time ! beneath my tread
   Unnumbered flowers, with laughing eye,
Are sprinkled o'er the teaming mead,
   Like stars that stud the midnight sky ;
Or, bathed in showers but lately o'er,
   They gleam afresh, in peerless pride,
Like gems along the ocean shore,
   When washed by the receding tide.

'Tis Summer-time ! the corn is seen,
   Luxuriant, waving far and near ;
The lambs are sporting on the green,
   The air is fragrant, soft, and clear ;
And Nature, with her sweet acclaim,
   Rich offerings on her altar lays,
And, while ascends the incense flame,
   She hymns her great Creator's praise.

'Tis Summer-time ! let us away,
   The joyous, fragrant, fields among,
To catch the linnet's thrilling lay,
   The lark's yet more transporting song ;
Or quaff the hill-side heathery air,
   And freely o'er the uplands roam,—
Loosed from the grasp of anxious care,—
   Where purer inspirations come ;

Where genius, with artistic skill,
   The while with Nature, face to face

With graphic power and noble will,

    Hath sketched her with a matchless grace ;

Lit up with pure poetic fire,

    How óft bard's noblest song hath been

Of Nature, in her rich attire,

    Her summer livery of green !

Oh ! be it mine, this Summer-time,

    To haunt the field, the wood, the plain !

To realize the true sublime

    Of Summer's sweet, inspiring, reign !

To kindle into wrapt delight,

    With glad, yet reverent, heart adore

The Author of this beauteous sight !

    God is His name for evermore.

ON THE DEATH OF KING WILLIAM IV.

HARK ! the wail, what sounds of sadness
  Fill the bounds of Britain's isle !
Silent is the voice of gladness ;
  Cancelled is Britannia's smile.

See ! in tears a nation bending
  Round our William's royal urn ;
Honest hearts with grief are rending,
  And thy sons, Britannia ! mourn.

There are loyal hearts within thee,
  Land of freedom, land of fame ;
In thy homes what prayers have blest thee !
  Round our hearths how sweet thy name !

Yes! there are whose prayers ascended,
　Monarch! while we owned thy sway,—
Prayers, with patriot fervour blended,
　All effectual, day by day.

But no more, throughout our isle,
　Peals the prayer for Britain's king;
Yet her sons shall weep awhile,
　And their wonted requiem bring.

Though with grief our hearts be smitten,
　Yet Victoria cheers our night;
Yes! her reign shall rise on Britain
　Beautiful as morning light.

Strength in undecaying beauty,
　Loyal zeal, and patriot fire,
Subjects brave, and prompt in duty,
　All to make thee great conspire.

Hail! Victoria, may the glory
　Of thy reign, and thy renown,
Be enrolled in future story,
　And descend to ages down!

Hail! Victoria, youthful sovereign,
　Scion of an ancient line,
Thrice ten thousand blessings, hovering
　O'er thee through thy days, be thine!

God Almighty still deliver
　Thee from foes, and shield thy head!
And prosperity, for ever,
　Through thy wide dominions spread!

THE FALL OF THE AMORITES.

WITH armour equipped, in the noon of their pride,
Did the kings of the Amorites vauntingly ride ;
And chariot and horsemen, awaiting the fight,
Were on Gibeon's plains at the opening light.

But the armies of Israel assailed them, and, lo !
The wrath of Jehovah came down on the foe ;
And they fell in their ranks, and their armour of mail,
By the blast of the Lord in the direful hail.

And the bones of the warrior, whose heart was of steel,
Unaccustomed the thrill of compassion to feel ;
Who was hot with revenge as he drew forth his blade,
Have long on the plains of Beth-horon been laid.

And the brow, unadorned with the conqueror's wreath,
Is dejected and pale with the impress of death ;
For the arm of Jehovah's unparalleled might,
Was signally bared in His Israel's sight.

And the sun on the wheels of his chariot was stayed ;
And the pale moon the sad demonstration surveyed :
Then her silvery rays fell on Ajalon grand,
And the night was like day throughout Gibeon's land.

TO A FRIEND.

DECEMBER'S sky with storm and tempest lowers,
   The withering blast sweeps through the leafless trees ;
The murky night, with fast descending showers,
   Finds me beside the fire, and laid at ease,
   Coining some lay with which a friend to please ;
A friend whom once I knew in other guise,
   But now at college, where no clowns can tease ;
And there, so snug among the learned and wise,
May well my humbling theme, and grovelling muse, despise.

And yet, I'll venture to salute thee still,
   Whom naught can lure from friendship's guileless ways ;
At least, I ween thy bosom feels the thrill,
   The generous flame, that through thy spirit plays,

And bids thee hail my simple, artless, lays ;

    Promptly, and cheerful, I'll present them here,

To calm thy breast, thy sinking hopes to raise,

    To soothe thy mind, thy solitude to cheer ;

    And woo thee all life's woes with fortitude to bear.

Too oft, alas ! our sombre spirits brood

    On future ills by fancy bred alone,

Gainsay the plan which heaven designs for good,

    And, blindly erring, counter to it run ;

And, ere the imagined conflict is begun,

    Sink in despair, and life before us grows

A dreary wilderness, where never sun,

    To gild the gloom, his cheering radiance shows ;

    But all around is dark ; beyond, o'erwhelming woes.

Still may those hopes which oft thy mind have stayed,

    When life was rough, and darkness veiled the skies,—

Hopes which reposed on heaven's sustaining aid,—

    Yield conscious solace 'mid the storms that rise !

The unseen hand that guides our destinies
    Hath led thee safely through unnumbered snares,
Brought to thy wants a thousand rich supplies,
    Redressed thy griefs, and lightened all thy cares :
    That hand shall guide thee still, even on to hoary hairs.

Sweet are the memories of mercies past,
    Of years gone by, but still with pleasure fraught ;
These, mind, tenacious, holdeth to the last,
    Firm as when first within its records wrought.
How will those scenes steal on the indulgent thought !—
    The home, the hearth, our youthful hopes and fears,
Friends, far removed, but ne'er to be forgot,
    And some consigned to silence and to tears,
    With all the hallowed scenes of long departed years.

The sacred ties which knit our souls as one,
    Our souls which, even yet, harmonious chime,
Are doubly strengthened by events long flown,
    Events of honest, artless, youthful prime.

How oft we've trod the vale at evening time,   '

While yet the day hung lingering in the west !

   Conversed, and mused, on nature's works sublime !

Heard the last songster sing itself to rest !

Ah ! then no weighty cares disturbed the youthful breast.

Say ! is the din of city life more dear,

   The hum of thousands mingling in thy gaze,

Than the loved cot, the quiet valley. where

   We shared those pleasures of our youthful days :

Or the sweet prattling, and the artless ways,

   Of the dear pledges of connubial vows ;

Thine own sweet home, ah ! that endearing phrase !

   The soothing counsel of thy faithful spouse,

   And all those sacred joys domestic life allows.

Absent from these, methinks thy spirits pine,

   And claim the sympathies a friend would yield ;

Well ! let thy thoughts on future good recline,

'Tis cheering hope will the prospective gild :

There are some flowers along life's chequered field ;

    Anticipate their sweets with hopeful breast ;

Thou yet shalt taste of joys, ere time shall wield

    His scythe, to lay thee in the grave to rest,

    And thy freed spirit rise to scenes among the blest.

ON THE

DESTRUCTION OF THE BRITISH FORCES

IN AFGHANISTAN, 1840.

THE swelling breeze had filled the sail,
   That whitened in the sun ;
The noble ship had anchor weighed,
   Her destined course to run :
And there, embarked, the soldier stood,
   Erect his manly head ;
Doomed in a distant land, for mine
   Alas ! his blood to shed.

But ah ! what feelings thrilled his soul,
   As round his looks were cast,
And saw the land that gave him birth

Fade on his sight, at last !
The land whose spells his manly breast
Had owned with falling tears,
Where childhood played, and manhood met
The friends of former years.

Then there were thoughts of blissful days
That o'er his spirit came,
When in a father's smile he learned
That sweet, endearing, name :
The home, the hearth, the grateful tear
That spake a mother's joy,
As rose her morn and evening prayer
For him, her darling boy.

At length, by breeze and billow borne,
Another land he gains,
Where suns, and cloudless skies, are bright
O'er Afghanistan's plains :
But ah ! to him the land of death ;

Her soil hath drunk his gore ;
He bravely with his comrades fell,
· He fell, to rise no more.

No more the sire, with hoary hairs,
   Shall start to clasp his son ;
Or she that o'er his cradle bent,
   And hushed her wailing one.
His plumèd head is lowly laid ;
   He lies the sod beneath ;
A soldier's grave hath o'er him closed ;
   He sleeps the sleep of death.

O Albion ! while less favoured realms
   Shall calmly rest in peace,
Must thy sweet hearths be scarred by war ?
   Their matchless joys decrease ?
How many homes are cheerless now !
   How many widows mourn !

And hark ! that infant's plaintive wail,
  " When will my sire return ?"

O God of Britain ! shield her sons,
  Whose valour never waned ;
Teach her her prowess, and her might,
  By man is not maintained ;
A hand unseen shall wield the sword,
  Her destinies shall guide ;
Lay prostrate at her feet her foes,
  And blast them in their pride.

HIS CREED IS BETTER FAR THAN THINE.

HAST thou within thy breast a flame,
 A quenchless, an immortal, fire ?
An essence, yes, that still the same
 Must glow when ages shall expire ?

It may be, thou hast this denied,
 Or doubts of it have troubled thee ;
My fellow man ! then, turn aside,
 Look here, and pause : reflect with me.

Beholdest thou that humble grave ?
 Therein was laid, with many tears,
Him whom no human aid could save,
 Cut off, in prime of strength and years.

The mountain pine hast thou not seen,

. Which hurricanes around had played,

A monument sublime when e'en,

All blasted, it on earth was laid ?

So was it with this noble form ;

This manly, this majestic, frame,

Wrecked by the pestilential storm,

The dire disease, that quickly came.

Within that grave I saw him laid,

And much his aged father mourned ;

But, when the last sad rites were paid,

And dust to mouldering dust returned ;

I saw that man of hoary hairs ;

Amid his grief he stood sublime,

Hope brightly beaming through his tears,

Pointing beyond the bounds of time.

His creed was, that the grave must be
   To life, immortal life, the way ;
That death is immortality,
   The passage to unending day.

Beneath the weight of years and grief,
   And dense, and deep, surrounding gloom,
This gave him comfort, brought relief,
   And lit the darkness of the tomb.

So, when the midnight reign is past,
   That closes round the traveller's way,
He hails the morn, it breaks at last,
   The prelude to encircling day.

When thou, with anguish, did'st consign
   To death's inexorable power
Thy bosom friend, what hopes were thine,
   To cheer thee in that solemn hour?

Did then thy creed with light surround
   The grave?—that dim and dreary sphere;—
Or was it darkness, all profound,
   With not a ray of hope to cheer?

If so, then he whose faith can show
   A hope, and fortitude, divine,
In life or death, in weal or woe,
   His creed is better far than thine.

.

TO MY SISTER,

ON HER BIRTHDAY.

THE flower that drinks the evening dew,
　And sweetly scents the morning air,
That blooms in colours rich and new,
　And flourishes awhile so fair,
Shall fade before the direful blast,
　An emblem meet of youth's decay ;
So soon the spring of life is past,
　And its meridian fades away.

But time's eventful course may bring
　A few more years thy youth to crown ;
And, like the balmy breath of spring,
　Which gives the fleeting year renown,

H

So youth, improved, shall give to age
  A lustre that shall ne'er decay :
And every birthday shall presage
  Honours that ne'er shall fade away.

Though few the birthdays thou hast seen,
  My sister, in this world of tears ;
Yet sorrow hath thy portion been,
  And griefs have multiplied with years :
I saw thee drain affliction's cup,
  While yet youth's rising sun did shine ;
Nor scarce remained one ray of hope,
  That health would ever more be thine.

Since then, a few more years have passed,
  And many, I hope, thou yet wilt see ;
And, as thy life shall run to waste,
  More joyous may each birthday be !
And, when thy day is nearly done,

And evening's shades o'er thee prevail,

Be glorious, then, thy setting sun !

Thy portion, bliss that ne'er shall fail !

THE ORPHANS.

THE sun his dying splendour
  All gloriously did shower
On lofty spire, and pinnacle,
  One quiet evening hour ;
No sounds discordant mingled,
  As on my way I hied ;
And naught the woe betokened
  So soon to be descried.

At length, I reached a cottage
  Where scarce a sunbeam glowed,
So dreary was its aspect,
  So cheerless its abode ;
A widow, poor and wretched,

With orphan children, were
Its inmates,—when I saw it,—
In want, and in despair :

One hapless boy had fallen,
  All prostrate, on the ground,—
Had swooned away, exhausted,
  And bleeding from a wound :
He lay, poor helpless infant !
  As if in death's embrace,
With agony depicted
  Upon his pallid face.

Another, so afflicted,
  So wasted, thin, and pale,
Lay, blasted like a flower
  Before the ruthless gale.
A few brief hours subsided,

And then the struggle ceased ;
　The stricken one lay quiet,
　　The sufferer was released.

The mother,—she had hastened,
　With misery half wild,
To seek, if she might find it,
　Some succour for her child :
Her heart was anguish-stricken,
　Such anguish who can name ?
None but a mother knows it ;
　She who has felt the same.

Six children, poor, afflicted,
　Were in that wretched shed ;
No father's hand to shield them,
　Or earn them daily bread ;
Life's wilderness before them ;

And never more will they
Receive a father's counsel,
 Along life's weary way.

When snares their path encircle,
 Unbridled passions reign,
Or human frailties mingle
 The mastery to gain ;
When life is rough and dreary,
 And sorrows cloud the way,
Who then shall guide the fatherless,
 And be the orphans' stay ?

O Thou ! in pity boundless,
 The orphans' changeless friend,
What hand but Thine can shield them ?
 Guide, succour, save, defend ?
O God ! in mercy help Thou

THE ORPHANS.

The orphan in distress !
Up-raise the crushed in spirit;
　Relieve their wretchedness.

Though earth is clad in beauty,
　And from the heavens the light
Is richly streaming earthward,
　So beautiful and bright ;
What souls are dark with sorrow !
　What bosoms heave with grief !
How many broken-hearted
　Are sighing for relief !

The affluent, surrounded
　With luxury, and ease,
And every creature-comfort
　The appetite to please,
Alas ! are often mindless

Of those who sigh for bread, —
The widow, and the orphan,
   Half naked, and half fed.

Though wealth may claim distinction,
   And thousands, every day,
Will cringe, and fall, before it,
   And homage to it pay,
When even its possessor
   Is poor in all beside,
Too poor with what is noble
   Ever to be allied ;—

The sigh, the wail of anguish
   Ne'er move their callous breast,
Nor sympathy, nor pity,
   Dwells there for the distressed ;
No sigh, no tale, of misery

That ever may be told,
　Allays, one single moment,
　　Their ceaseless thirst for gold.

That wretched orphan, trailing
　In rags along the street,
All deeply foul with mire,
　With bare, and bleeding, feet,
No friend, no food, no shelter
　That may for home atone;
His misery and anguish
　Might move a heart of stone.

The woes of earth are many :
　The sorrows of my race,
O hapless fellow mortal !
　Are stamped upon thy face :
The eye where pity lingers

Is wont the tear to shed,
To mark the path of suffering
    Humanity must tread.

The truly noble hearted,
    The generous in mind,
Would fain assuage the miseries
    That press upon mankind :
But miser, muck-worm, mortals,
    So dwarfed in soul, and poor,
Would even spurn the orphan,
    Who begs from door to door.

ON THE PROPOSED

REPEAL OF THE NAVIGATION LAWS,

IN 1847.

IT has often been said, and there are who yet teach,
That an Englishman's heart through his throat you must reach :
His humour, and courage, depend, they declare,
On the rum and beefsteaks that may fall to his share.

Though self-preservation be nature's loved way,
And the doctrine just named is correct, you may say:
Yet others will firmly maintain that John Bull
Will contend for his rights, whether empty, or full.

But the worst of all evils that John has to dread,
So Brougham, Disraeli, and Stanley, have said,
Is hatched, and is pending, and will be revealed
If the laws of Protection are ever repealed.

Our commerce at sea, and our maritime force,
'Tis alleged on all hands, will be crippled, and worse ;
That John, the first maritime power in the world,
Will soon from this lofty position be hurled.

The nations of Europe will not entertain
This matter, 'tis said, so will pocket the gain ;
And, though the example by England be set,
They will not espouse it, or copy it, yet.

There is truth, we believe, and philosophy, here ;
And time, and a trial, will make this appear.
You speak of philosophy ! can it be so ?
Can a measure be bad, and yet popular too ?

Has the matter not ably been handled throughout,
By men of great tact, in the Senate, and out ?
And has it been shown, by philosophy's aid,
That the measure will injure our maritime trade ?

The proof now demanded is this : it is plain,
That nations, in general, are anxious for gain,
So much so that, like individual man,
They grasp at the profit whenever they can.

And hence, from analogy, people should learn,
That the nations around us will quickly discern,
When the measure propounded is law, as too soon
It may be, it will yield them a very great boon.

Hence, then, they will prize it as bringing them gain,
And from the like measure, will, doubtless, refrain ;
For, while the concession is all on our side,
Theirs will be the profit : this can't be denied.

If only their laws they would also repeal,
And so deal with us as we with them deal ;
Why, then would the benefit mutual be,
And all on the subject proposed would agree.

John Bull doth, however, a generous trait,

In matters to state appertaining, display,

A sort of large-heartedness, prone to transcend

All regard for himself, or the sum he may spend.

It is with him just now, as it has been of yore,

To battle for others, and then pay the score :

'Tis generous certainly, noble, and brave,

'Tis very magnanimous thus to behave ;

But is it judicious, or prudent, or wise,

This one-sided scheme to suggest, or devise ?

We can but predict,—may it never prove true !—

John Bull for this measure will certainly rue.

It is argued by some that we must lead the way,

And set the example, without more delay,

In all things relating to progress ; and, though

We may suffer awhile, 'twill not always be so.

Moreover, 'tis said that the fame, and renown,
Will be ours, and go to posterity down ;
That this, to a people so noble, and strong,
Is a motive sufficient to prompt us along.

This seems rather specious, but does not apply
To the matter in question ; do you ask why ?
Why, simply because other nations will say
Our interest lies quite in the opposite way.

How think you will look our brave tars, all the while,
On their mess of frog-soup in the foreigner's style ?
Think you not that the quid will have many a turn,
While Jack's weather-eye will with enmity burn ?

O England ! old England, of ancient renown,
Must thy sons' noble spirit be broken thus down ?
Must the shaft of destruction thus at thee be hurled ?—
Whose prowess is echoed through all the wide world.

Still may the proud ships of our ocean-girt isle
Yet cause her in riches, and commerce, to smile !
And her mariners, cradled in tempest, shall ride,
Victorious as ever, upon the blue tide.

Act nobly thy part ! on thy rulers depend !
There are yet those to guide thee, and God shall befriend;
" Britannia for ages shall yet rule the waves,
And BRITONS SHALL NEVER, NO, NEVER BE SLAVES !"

TO THE DAISY.

HOW shall I speak of thee, sweet flower ?
　　Since mighty bards thy praise have sung ;
And Burns, with glowing, glorious, power,
　　Hath from his lyre such numbers flung
That, but for thine alluring spell,
　　My humbler muse would droop her wing,
Nor would she ever aim to tell
　　The memories thou hast power to bring.

Didst thou not bloom amid the bowers
　　Depicted still in childhood's page,
And tinge with golden hues those hours
　　That fade not with the snows of age ?
Around my cottage-home wert thou,
　　With thy compeers, like pearls from heaven ;
Sweet diadems in nature's brow,
　　Lit up, and to my childhood given.

Bathed in the radiant beams of light,

    And late with genial dews refreshed,

How oft thy looks rejoiced my sight!

    Of all the flowers, I loved thee best :

Thou beauteous, waving, gem! so free

    When storms arouse the troubled air,

An angel's wing might shelter thee,

    As not unworthy of his care.

Thou liftest up thy little head,

    And grace, and comeliness, are thine;

And, in thy looks, who can but read

    A language simple, yet divine!

It speaks of Him who did create

    Thy lovely form, and bade thee spring,

In living bloom, to decorate

    The green earth with thy blossoming.

Hadst thou thy birth in Eden's clime ?

    And didst thou feel the gentle air,

All tremulous, at evening time,

I 2

When angels' wings were hovering near ?
And didst thou drink the dews that fell,
    And bud in Eden's bowers so sweet ?
Oh ! tell me, I beseech thee, tell,
    Thou beauteous flower beneath my feet !

Suffice for me thy looks, so mild,
    Flashed on me in the light of day.
When I,—an artless, playful, child,—
    Roamed freely o'er the fields away :
Those looks allured, and charmed me, then ;
    And still, where'er thy form I see,
On moor, or mead, in grove, or glen,
    More beautiful are they for thee.

I would not bruise thy lowly head,
    Nor mar thy graceful form : of old,
The bard of Scotia did that deed,
    Then in immortal numbers told :
He gladly would have sought thy weal,

And sighed to crush thy early birth,
For poets, oft, are keen to feel,
    And love all beauteous things of earth.

Thou art arrayed in modest bloom,
    A Summer's sun is o'er thee now ;
But soon, full soon, alas ! will come
    The Wintry blast, to scathe thy brow :
For fate decrees both I and thou
    Must rue the bleak, tempestuous, hour,
Beneath the storms of time must bow
    When skies are black, and tempests lower.

And many a dark, and sunless, day,
    And tempest-hour, have o'er us rolled,
Yet here thou art, in glad array,
    And I to greet thee as of old :
While He who gave us life, and form,
    Who framed the earth, the tenderest blade,
Hath oft allayed the raging storm,
    And raised us up, when lowly laid.

And now, farewell ! I must away,
    Life's noble purpose to fulfil,
Pursue with earnest aim its way,
    With firm, and unrelaxing, will ;
And may'st thou live and bloom : and, when
    Shall come the bleak, tempestuous, hour ;
Oh ! may'st thou find some shelter, then,
    Thou blitheful, beauteous, little flower.

Yes ! thou wilt bloom when life, with me,
    With its conflicting scenes, are o'er ;
And genial suns will visit thee,
    When I behold thy form no more ;
And, when the verdant grass shall wave,
    And leafy woods with warbles ring,
Oh ! do thou then my humble grave
    Adorn, thou precious, darling, thing !

THE OLD SOLDIER.

THE sun had crimsoned all the west,
   The day was near its close,
And evening gently drawing round
   The curtain of repose :
Inimitable beauty seemed
   On all below impressed,
And sweetly were the feathered choir
   Singing themselves to rest.

At this auspicious hour, I sought,
   In meditative mood,
Some respite from tumultuous life,
   Some place of solitude.
Beside my path, as on I passed,
   A poor old man reclined ;
His scanty locks, all silvery white,
   Were floating in the wind.

His eye was dim ; and care, and want,
   And age, had on him told ;
He spake of eighty years, or more,
   That o'er his head had rolled,
And, like an ancient tree that falls
   When time hath sealed its doom,
This venerable man appeared
   Just ready for the tomb.

Life's long, and toilsome, day, with him,
   Was nearing to its close,
And, travel-worn, this aged man
   Sighed for the grave's repose ;
Yet meek submission, patience, trust,
   Hope, fortitude divine,
His countenance, serene, pourtrayed,
   As it was turned on mine.

Philosophy may proudly scorn,
   The infidel despise
The good man's inward solace, hope,

His hold upon the skies :
His faith, his trust, is in the Lamb,
    The one oblation made,
His comfort this amid life's woes,
    And death's approaching shade.

The hard realities of life,—
    Privation, labour, pain,—
This aged man had oft endured,
    On battle-field, and main ;
In manhood's prime, amid the brave,
    The battle's dread array,
He fought, he bled, for England's weal,
    Where War's red carnage lay.

The current of his soldier-life,
    Impetuous, and strong,
At length was calmed, and changed, when years
    Had rolled their course along :
And, as he sought his father-land,

Where friend, and kindred, slept,
　And saw his cottage-home again,
　　He sat him down, and wept.

He wept that now no father's smile,
　No mother's fond embrace,
Awaited him, for both were borne
　To their last resting place :
The loved companions of his youth
　Were scattered wide, or laid
Within the precincts of the grave,
　Beneath the elm-trees' shade.

And, as he lingered near the spot
　Where once his childhood grew,
And all the past was reproduced
　So vividly to view,
He breathed a prayer sincere to heaven,
　A suppliant groan, a sigh,
That he forgiveness might obtain,
　And then, at home, might die.

This man of valour, stern and tried,
　That oft the foe withstood,
And firmly braved the blast of war,—
　The shock, the charge of blood,—
Now, with an anxious, broken heart,
　With misery oppressed,
Sought, till he found, the heavenly balm
　That healed his bleeding breast.

A radiant beam of light divine
　Dispelled his midnight gloom,
Illumed the wilderness of life,
　And shone upon the tomb.
The Christian's armour thence he wore,
　And, counting all things loss,
He fought, the victory to win,—
　A soldier of the Cross.

And now, his sun was going down,
　Serene, and broad, 'and bright,
And, at the evening time of life,

There beamed the heavenly light ;
And, leaning on his staff, he said
    "My conflict now is brief,
Life's passage has with me been rough
    Across this world of grief :

"I've in my country's service bled,
    Amid the battle's roar ;
My sole reward the victor's joy,
    When the hard fight was o'er :
Enlisted in my Saviour's cause,
    How poor the service given !
Yet here, how rich is my reward !—
    To be prolonged in Heaven."

He paused, with deep emotion swayed ;
    His tears then copious fell,
Which more of inward joy revealed
    Than even words could tell :
And, contemplating death as near,

Like Israel of old
He with his fathers fain would rest
  Beneath the parent mould.

"How oft when I, at duty's call,
  In distant spheres did roam,
My thoughts," he said, "would dwell on this,—
  On kindred, and on home !
And, God be praised ! that I, at last,
  Shall lay my bones with those
Of loved ones in my native land,
  In undisturbed repose."

And, as upon his face I looked,—
  Time-furrowed, pale, and wan,—
Instinctive nature in me urged
  The Brotherhood of Man :
The common sympathies we feel,
  Of action, thought, or mind,
God, in His wisdom, gave us these
  To benefit our kind.

DEPARTED HOURS.

AH ! think not that departed hours
    Have left no trace behind,
Like dewdrops, kissed from Summer flowers,
    Or echoes on the wind :
For still, in memory's page appears,
    In prominent array,
The record of preceded years,
    For ever passed away.

'Mid silence, or the busy hum
    Of life,—in every place,—
The memories of the past will come
    To meet us, face to face ;
Will come, to yield us joy or grief,
    As acts of days gone by
Shall colour out in bold relief,
    And good, or ill, imply.

The clouds, all tinged with golden hues
    That round our childhood spread,
Have disappeared like Summer dews,
    And are for ever fled ;
But still the memory doth remain
    Of all this fairy scene ;
In retrospect it lives again,
    Though years have rolled between.

No more the patriarch of the vale,
    Beside his cottage door,
Shall greet our childhood with the tale
    That charmed us oft, of yore ;
But ah ! to memory still endeared,
    Nor may we soon forget
How beautiful the scene appeared ;
    The vision lingers yet.

No more the warm, endearing, smile,
    That like a sunbeam came,
And dried our infant tears the while

With its maternal flame ;—
Though now no more, as when of old.
    That smile be on us cast,
Its spells no language may unfold,
    Endearing all the past.

Departed hours, who may forget ? '
    In retrospect arrayed,
What visions linger round them yet,
    All tinged with light, or shade !
The hallowed scenes of early years,
    The forms, and faces, there,
Are yet beheld, through smiles, or tears,
    All fresh, as once they were.

The day, with sunlit morning crowned,
    Oft yields to early gloom ;
And thorns, and flowers, spring up around
    The pathway to the tomb ;
And, where along life's road we've passed,

DEPARTED HOURS

...s still there be
...urs, or hours o'er...
...nds, full suddenly.

...s not that departed hours
...t no trace behind,
...rops, kissed from Summer flowers.
...es on the wind :
...or eve, at noon, or night,
...soe'er we stray,
...mementoes meet the sight,
...s now passed away !

THE END.